The
Wicca
Source Book

Also by Gerina Dunwich

Candlelight Spells
The Magick of Candleburning
The Concise Lexicon of the Occult
Wicca Craft
The Secrets of Love Magick
The Wicca Spellbook
The Wicca Book of Days
The Wicca Garden
The Mystical World of Divination, Omens and Prophecy
    (forthcoming)
Cast a Spell: Wiccan Magick for Every Day of the Year
    (forthcoming)
Circle of Shadows: A Collection of Goddess-Inspired Poetry,
    Mystical Fantasies, and Magickal Verse
Words of the Cosmic Winds: Poems and Prayers of Pagan Power

The
Wicca
Source Book

A Complete Guide for
the Modern Witch

Gerina Dunwich

A CITADEL PRESS BOOK
PUBLISHED BY CAROL PUBLISHING GROUP

Carol Publishing Group Edition, 1997

A Citadel Press Book
Published by Carol Publishing Group
Citadel Press is a registered trademark of Carol Communications, Inc.

Editorial, sales and distribution, rights and permissions inquiries should be addressed to Carol Publishing Group, 120 Enterprise Avenue, Secaucus, N.J. 07094

In Canada: Canadian Manda Group, One Atlantic Avenue, Suite 105, Toronto, Ontario M6K 3E7

Carol Publishing Group books may be purchased in bulk at special discounts for sales promotions, fund-raising, or educational purposes. Special editions can be created to specifications. For details, contact Special Sales Department, Carol Publishing Group, 120 Enterprise Avenue, Secaucus, N.J. 07094

Manufactured in the United States of America
10 9 8 7 6 5 4 3 2

Library of Congress Cataloging-in-Publication Data

Dunwich, Gerina.
The Wicca source book : a complete guide for the modern witch / Gerina Dunwich.
p. cm.
"A Citadel Press book."
Includes bibliographical references and index.
ISBN 0-8065-1830-8 (pbk.)
1. Witchcraft—United States—Directories. 2. Neopaganism—United States—Directories. 3. New Age movement—United States—Directories. 4. Witches—United States—Directories. 5. Neopagans—United States—Directories. 6. New age persons—United States—Directories. I. Title.
BF1566.D88 1996
133.4'3'02573—dc20   96-27950
                                                                 CIP

With love do I dedicate this book to my mother, who gave me the precious gift of life; to Zen, who gave me the precious gift of love; to Wilva, who gave me the precious gift of friendship; and to Coven Mandragora, who gave me all of the above.

Special thanks and bright blessings to Al Jackter, Lee Prosser, Reed, Kathleen Kmen for her contributions to the Recommended Reading Section, and all else who participated in this project in one way or another. Thank you from the heart for helping to make this possible!

Contents

Introduction

Wicca, which is an Old English word meaning "wise," is a positive, Earth-oriented, nature religion with ancient roots that are pre-Christian. It gloriously celebrates the life force, encourages spiritual growth, and includes seasonal rites to attune oneself to the beauty, magick and love of Mother Nature and Goddess Earth.

Like the New Age spirituality movement, which has steadily been gaining momentum throughout the past ten years or so, Wicca is also growing, changing, and expanding. As more people become educated and enlightened to the ways of Wicca, the negative stereotypes and misconceptions associated with modern Witches and Pagans are gradually being shed.

Wicca is not a passing fad. It is a strong religion of light and love, both ancient and contemporary, that is here to stay.

This resource book was painstakingly put together for the purpose of connecting Wiccans, Pagans, and New Age spiritualists from around the world, and to help promote Wicca (the Craft of the Wise), Earth-Goddess religions, and all positive spiritual paths. All efforts have been made to produce a thorough and up-to-date compilation of listings to serve the entire Wiccan, Pagan, and New Age community as an invaluable resource directory. If I have accidentally left anyone out, or if any of the listings change or become discontinued by the time this book is published, I sincerely apologize and will do my best to correct any incomplete or incorrect information in future editions.

This book is made up of twelve important sections: organizations, Wiccan and Pagan churches, schools, books and publishers, periodicals, astrology, herbs, occult shops (listed by state), mail order, Pagan potpourri, a Who's Who of the Wiccan community, which features some of the most talented, well-known, accomplished, and respected members of the Wiccan community worldwide, and a Recommended Reading list. Many organizations and businesses are listed in more than one section, and all can be easily located in the alphabetically-arranged directory at the back of the book.

Whether you are searching for special occult supplies, a Pagan parenting group, the nearest Wiccan church, a Witchcraft correspondence course, a networking organization for gay and lesbian Witches, dream-catchers, mandrake roots, or astrological computer software, you are guaranteed to find it within the pages of this book!

If you are not presently listed in this book and wish to be considered for future editions, please write to me at the address below for a free application form. (To be listed there is no charge whatsoever.) If you are already listed, please keep me updated as to any changes regarding your listing(s). You may write to me in care of the publisher, or directly: Gerina Dunwich, P.O. Box 525, Fort Covington, New York 12937. (Please include a self-addressed stamped envelope.)

May the Goddess and the God in all of Their mysterious ways bless you with an abundance of Light, Love, Mirth, and Magick!

Blessed be

The
Wicca
Source Book

1

ORGANIZATIONS

In this section you will find the listings of many different organizations serving the needs of the Wiccan and Pagan communities around the world. Included are networking, contact, and support groups, Witches' covens, psychic and supernatural research societies, and various organizations who sponsor Pagan gatherings, provide education to the public, and protect the civil and religious rights of Wiccans, Pagans, and other "nonmainstream" religious groups.

This section also contains the listings of a number of Wiccan and Pagan churches. They are included here (instead of in the next chapter, which is devoted to legally-recognized churches) because either they are not yet legally recognized or their legal status was unknown at the time of this writing.

Arizona

Arizona Solitary Practitioners Empowerment Network (ASPEN)
P.O. Box 16651
Phoenix, Arizona 85011
(602) 242-0711

A regional networking organization for solitary practitioners of the Craft. No membership fees are required. Sponsors two retreats each year.

Desert Henge Coven
P.O. Box 40451
Tucson, Arizona 85717

Formed in 1982, this is one of the oldest covens in the state of Arizona. Following the Gardnerian tradition, it is divided into an Inner Court Coven and an Outer Court training group. Sponsors Arizona's oldest public class on Wicca and emphasizes the social interactions of coven as family. The current High Priest and High Priestess are Rik Johnson and Dianna Armentrout.

Pagan Arizona Network
P.O. Box 17933
Phoenix, Arizona 85011
(602) 230-5354

Networking for Pagan groups and solitary practitioners throughout the state of Arizona.

The Sacred Grove
16845 N. 29th Avenue, no. 1346
Phoenix, Arizona 85023

An international referral network for solitary practitioners and groups of various Wiccan traditions.

Tucson Area Wiccan Network
P.O. Box 482
Tucson, Arizona 85702

A local referral network for Wiccans, Pagans, and all followers of the Wiccan Rede. Provides "social, spiritual, and educational interactions."

California

American Druidic Church
c/o Jay and Patricia Tibbles
P.O Box 2642
Fontana, California 92334

Ancient Religions Society
2265 Westwood Boulevard
Los Angeles, California 90064
(213) 506-8670

Local and regional referrals for groups and individuals who follow the Old Ways.

Ancient Religions Society
1157½ W. 30th Street, Box B-3
Los Angeles, California 90007
(213) 856-2824

A newly-formed religious organization run by students at UCLA that provides education, information, networking, and social contacts for Wiccans, Pagans, and other individuals belonging to nonmainstream religions.

Bay Area Pagan Assemblies
P.O. Box 850
Fremont, California 94537
(408) 559-GAIA

A local referral network and nonprofit organization servicing the San Francisco area's Pagan community. Publishes *Pagan Muse and World Report.*

Branching
P.O. Box 3155
East Hampton, New York 11937

414 E. Cedar, No. 9
Burbank, California 91501

"A support group for solitary Wiccans and Pagans, Branching is a group of people on a positive path who network by mail. Membership directory is offered. Survey done by members tells us what our members' interests are. We share ceremonial themes, rituals, lunar workings, long-distance magick, healing." Publishes an occasional newsletter.

Church of All Worlds Central
P.O. Box 1542
Ukiah, California 95482
(707) 463-1432

The oldest Neo-Pagan church in the United States, founded in 1962, legally incorporated in 1968. Inspired by the science fiction novel *Stranger in a Strange Land*, by Robert Heinlein. The first Pagan church to be legally incorporated in Australia. Over fifty "nests" worldwide. Holds monthly meetings and owns festival lands in California and Kentucky. Write for additional information.

Covenant of the Goddess
P.O. Box 1226
Berkeley, California 94701

An international council network and the largest federation of covens and solitary elders from different Wiccan traditions. They sponsor a newsletter and festival, and also issue ministerial credentials.

Earth Religions Integrative Network
P.O. Box 482
Mount Shasta, California 96067

This is a local referral network that sponsors classes and rituals for the Sabbats.

The Educational Society for Pagans
115 W. California Boulevard, no. 161
Pasadena, California 91105
(818) 583-9353 (twenty-four-hour recorded information)

Formerly the Pallas Society. Provides educational resources and networking. Promotes public outreach work for Southern California Wiccans and Pagans.

Elderflower
P.O. Box 31627
San Francisco, California 94131
(916) 558-0607

Organizes the annual Womenspirit Festivals. Write or call for more information and the current registration fees.

The Foundation for Shamanic Studies
Dr. Michael Harner, director
P.O. Box 1939
Mill Valley, California 94942
(415) 380-8282; Fax: (415) 380-8416

The Index
P.O. Box 1646
Santa Cruz, California 95061
(408) 427-5347

A local referral network for the Pagan community of Santa Cruz and the central California coast. For additional information, please send a self-addressed stamped envelope.

Moon Lodge Network
204½ E. Broadway
Costa Mesa, California 92627
(714) 548-0551

An international referral network and council for women interested in spiritual visioning and healing. It also provides workshops and annual ceremonies, and publishes a biannual journal.

Neo-African Network
c/o Technicians of the Sacred
1317 N. San Fernando Boulevard, Suite 310
Burbank, California 91504

An "informal" international network for followers of Voudoun, Santeria, Macumba, Thelemic Voudoun, and the Family Traditions. No membership fees are required.

New Wiccan Church
P.O. Box 162046
Sacramento, California 95816

An international federation of British Traditional Wicca with branches in several states and overseas. To receive information regarding membership, networking, or contact referrals, send a self-addressed stamped envelope along with two first-class stamps.

Pagan Broadcasting System
P.O. Box 16025
North Hollywood, California 91615

A computer bulletin board.

Pagan/Occult/Witchcraft Special Interest Group of Mensa
P.O. Box 9336
San Jose, California 95157

Support Abused Wiccans
201 W. Moneta
Bakersfield, California 93308

The Susan B. Anthony Women's Spirituality Education Forum, Inc.
P.O. Box 11363
Oakland, California 94611

Women's Spiritual Network and Database of Central California and Beyond
P.O. Box 3903
Salinas, California 93912

Women's Spirituality Forum
P.O. Box 11363
Oakland, California 94611
(510) 444-7724

A nonprofit, Goddess-oriented organization providing a lecture series, classes, cable television shows, spiral dances, and retreats. For additional information, please contact ZsuZsanna Budapest.

United We Circle
3208 Cahuenga Boulevard
West Hollywood, California 90068
(213) 876-4032

A local Witchcraft organization made up of members of the Los Angeles Wiccan Religious Community. Organizes letter-writing campaigns and press conferences.

Colorado

Earth Spirit Pagans
P.O. Box 1965
Colorado Springs, Colorado 80901
(800) 731-2650

An órganization dedicated to the preservation and continued vitality of Pagan religions and cultures. Provides a caring and nurturing environment for practitioners of Pagan paths, including regular rituals, classes, workshops, handfastings, Wiccanings and memoriams. Donations are tax-deductable.

The Web
P.O. Box 1871
Boulder, Colorado 80306
(303) 939-8832

A local referral network for Pagans and Witches seeking Craft-related activities, education, and "Pagan-friendly" professionals and support.

The Witching Well Education and Research Center
P.O. Box 1490
Idaho Springs, Colorado 80452

An organization dedicated to education concerning the Ancient Arts. To receive one of its free educational pamphlets, please send a self-addressed stamped envelope along with your request.

World Pagan Network
721 N. Hancock Avenue
Colorado Springs, Colorado 80903
(719) 632-7249

A networking and contact resource for the seeking Pagan. WPN is staffed by volunteers from around the world. If you are seeking Pagans in your community or are moving around the world, WPN can help you. Request for information should include the following: name, address, country, and area where you are looking for contacts. There is no fee for this service. If you would like to volunteer as a contact, please write for details. Contact: Chris West.

Connecticut

Craft Wise
P.O. Box 457
Botsford, Connecticut 06404
(203) 374-6475

Sponsors Pagan gatherings across the United States and Canada. The object of the gatherings is to bring quality instruction and rituals to communities across the country, sharing knowledge and skills with those who are isolated or simply not in touch with trained teachers. The group's purpose is fundamentally that of an open teaching community clustered in the alternative religions and the occult community.

New Wiccan Church of Connecticut
N.W.C.
c/o Lady of the Brook
P.O. Box 11
Plainfield, Connecticut 06374

Witches Information Network
415 Campbell Avenue
West Haven, Connecticut 06516
(203) 932-1193

A local referral council established to educate the public about Witches. Also provides coven and group referrals.

Florida

Alachua Pagan Alliance
P.O. Box 12625
Gainesville, Florida 32604

Provides referrals for various Earth-centered and Goddess traditions, as well as public education on the practice of Paganism.

Crone's Cradle Conserve
P.O. Box 1207
Citra, Florida 32113

Danae's Sun
P.O. Box 47384
Jacksonville, Florida 32247

An international mail network for teens and young adults from all positive, nature-honoring spiritual paths. Free membership includes letter exchange and newsletter. For more information, contact Dana Solis.

Life Spring
2190 Traymore Road
Jacksonville, Florida 32207
(904) 396-9637

Provides local networking for Pagans in the state of Florida. Write or call for additional information.

Pagan Allied Network International, Inc.
P.A.N.
P.O. Box 290864
Temple Terrace, Florida 33687
(904) 521-3647

An international council that sponsors Sabbat celebrations that are open to all Pagans. Provides international networking for groups and individuals.

Southeast Florida Pagan Coalition
P.O. Box 848896
Hollywood, Florida 33084
(407) 395-5325; (305) 923-4192

Pagan networking and community ritual. All groups and covens are welcome.

Wiccan Religious Cooperative of Florida, Inc.
3936 S. Semoran Boulevard, Suite 116
Orlando, Florida 32822
(407) 657-2182; (407) 725-4316

Provides discussion groups, educational classes, seminars, worship circles, work groups, cultural and social activities, and networking opportunities for the Wiccan community.

Georgia

Universal Federation of Pagans
P.O. Box 6006
Athens, Georgia 30604
(706) 369-6813

A worldwide Pagan association. For membership requirements and application, please send a self-addressed stamped envelope.

Idaho

Earth Tribe-Pagan Division
P.O. Box 92
Burley, Idaho 83318

An eclectic Wiccan and human rights organization emphasizing Pagan religious freedom. Legally incorporated in the state of Idaho in 1993 and serving as the Idaho chapter of Witches Against Religious Discrimination.

Indiana

Indiana Witches Against Religious Discrimination
WARD
c/o Diana Barnett
7317 W. 134th Court
Cedar Lake, Indiana 46303
(219) 374-7245

A statewide Witchcraft and Wiccan antidefamation network, founded in 1993.

Elf Lore Family (ELF)
Box 1082
Bloomington, Indiana 47402

A nonprofit organization providing Pagan networking, craftworking, survival skills, forest care, and woodland folklore. It maintains a nature sanctuary, survival education center, and a woodland meeting ground known as Lothlorien.

The Inkwell Circle
P.O. Box 4193
Anderson, Indiana 46013

A national mail network for Wiccans, Pagans, and others of a positive spiritual path.

Pagan Educational Network
P.O. Box 1364
Bloomington, Indiana 47402

A nonprofit Pagan organization providing national networking, volunteering, education, and letter writing. One-year membership: $12.00. Write for a membership form and additional information.

Illinois

Ghost Research Society
Dale Kaczmarek, president
P.O. Box 205
Oak Lawn, Illinois 60454
(312) 425-5163

Midwest Pagan Council
P.O. Box 160
Western Springs, Illinois 60558
(312) 767-1113

A regional and national council of Midwest Pagan groups. Sponsors the Pan Pagan Festival and other events, and publishes a newsletter.

Potlatch
P.O. Box 4674
Chicago, Illinois 60680

An education and communications organization "honoring ecology, community service, and natural spirituality." For more information, contact Lee A. Allen.

Iowa

Iowa Wiccan-Pagan Network
c/o Lady Isadora
P.O. Box 2483
Des Moines, Iowa 50311

Provides referrals to covens and solitary practitioners of the Craft in Des Moines and central Iowa. Holds monthly potluck meetings, discussions, and occasional Sabbat rituals.

Network of Pagan Midwives
2000 N. Court, no. 13-G
Fairfield, Iowa 52556
(515) 472-0751

Provides networking, support, education, outreach, and references for Pagan individuals seeking a midwife or an apprenticeship. Write or call for free information.

Kansas

Heartland Spiritual Alliance
P.O. Box 3407
Kansas City, Kansas 66103
(816) 561-6111

Founded in 1986, this Pagan organization provides a monthly Spirit Circle for educational purposes and networking. They also sponsor the annual Heartland Spirit Festival for Pagans of all spiritual paths.

Kentucky

The Rosemoon Guild
P.O. Box 23675
Lexington, Kentucky 40523

Provides networking, workshops, and social activities for Pagans of various spiritual paths. Write for additional information and a membership application.

Maryland

Coalition for Pagan Religious Rights
c/o The Turning Wheel Bookstore
8039-A Ritchie Highway
Pasadena, Maryland 21122

A newly-formed group of Witches, Druids, Mystic Christians, Shamans, and other Pagans from the Washington and Baltimore area. Write for more information.

Free Spirit Alliance
P.O. Box 25242
Baltimore, Maryland 21229
(301) 604-6049

A regional network for Pantheistic groups of individuals from different paths in the mid-Atlantic area. Sponsors the Free Spirit Festival and publishes *Free Spirit Rising*. For more information and a list of area groups, send a self-addressed stamped envelope.

Womanspirit Web
P.O. Box 513
Kensington, Maryland 20895
(301) 589-4635

A local and regional network promoting the practices and goals of women's spirituality and planetary healing. Write or call for additional information.

Massachusetts

Boston South Shore and Plymouth Area Pagan Network
P.O. Box 335
Boston University Station
Boston, Massachusetts 02215

A networking group for local Wiccans, Pagans, and other magickal folks. For more information, contact Arachne.

Covenant of Unitarian Universalist Pagans (CUUPS)
P.O. Box 640
Cambridge, Massachusetts 02140
(617) 547-6465

An international network of Unitarian Universalists and others who follow the positive paths of Neo-Paganism and Earth-centered spirituality. Publisher of *Pagan Nuus* and other resource materials.

Earth Spirit
P.O. Box 365
Medford, Massachusetts 02155
(617) 395-1023; Fax: (617) 396-5066

A national networking organization serving the Pagan community. Provides lectures, workshops, concerts, seasonal open circles, legal handfastings, spiritual counseling, and more. Send a self-addressed stamped envelope to receive an information brochure.

Full Circle CSCD
   37 Clark Road
   Cummington, Massachusetts 01026
   (413) 634-0262

   Provides four Pagan gatherings annually, a quarterly newsletter with a calendar of regional events, public and private ceremonies and instruction, a networking service, workshops, women's moon lodge, and various other personalized services. Call or write for more information.

MIT Pagan Students Association
   c/o Association of Student Activities
   MIT
   77 Massachusetts Avenue
   Cambridge, Massachusetts 02139

The Pathway of the Rose
   P.O. Box 698
   Ayer, Massachusetts 01432

   An international referral network and "phone tree" for Pagans of various traditions.

The Thomas Morton Alliance
   51 Plover Road
   Quincy, Massachusetts 02169

   A Pagan political organization. Write for more information.

University of Massachusetts Pagan Students Association
   P.O. Box 117
   Student Union Building, University of Massachusetts, Amherst, Massachusetts 01003

Western Massachusetts Pagan Alliance
   1500 Main Street
   P.O. Box 15083
   Springfield, Massachusetts 01115
   (413) 746-1432

   A regional network for Pagans of different backgrounds and traditions. Provides workshops, lectures, concerts, and open circles.

The Witches League for Public Awareness (WLPA)
P.O. Box 8736
Salem, Massachusetts 01971
Antidefamation organization.

Michigan

Ancient Altars
2420 Faunce Student Services
Western Michigan University, Box 2
Kalamazoo, Michigan 49008

A spiritual registered student organization on the Western Michigan University campus. Provides networking, education, and support to the Pagan community.

Great Lakes Pagan Council
P.O. Box 8281
Roseville, Michigan 48066
(313) 871-9252

Provides information on Pagan events and activities, promotes community and networking, and works to educate the public about Pagan ways. For more information, contact Oberon.

Magical Education Center of Ann Arbor
P.O. Box 7727
Ann Arbor, Michigan 48107

Pegasus
3767 W. Michigan Avenue
Battle Creek, Michigan 49017
(616) 963-4353

A regional referral council and "phone tree" for Witches belonging to different traditions.

Sanctuary of the Silver Moon
P.O. Box 6052
Grand Rapids, Michigan 49516

Networks with Pagan solitary practitioners and also incarcerated Pagans. For more information, contact Storm.

Web-KORE
   4217 Highland Road, Box 213
   Waterford, Michigan 48328

An eclectic Neo-Pagan and Wiccan group, founded in 1989. It provides monthly meetings and sponsors four large annual rituals.

Minnesota

The Henge of Keltria
   P.O. Box 48369
   Minneapolis, Minnesota 55448

A nonprofit religious corporation to foster and practice the spiritual and cultural teachings of Celtic Earth-based religions, particularly Keltrian Druidism. They have member groves in both the United States and Canada, and are the publishers of *Keltria: Journal of Druidism and Celtic Magick* and other Neo-Pagan Druid resources. For additional information, send a self-addressed stamped envelope or e-mail Keltria @ AOL.COM.

Omphalos Pagan Community Center
   P.O. Box 26752
   St. Louis Park, Minnesota 55426
   (612) 458-7815

A local network serving the Pagan community in the Twin Cities metropolitan area.

Wiccan Church of Minnesota
   P.O. Box 6715
   Minnehaha Station
   Minneapolis, Minnesota 55406

Mississippi

Rainbow Link
   P.O. Box 1218
   Greenville, Mississippi 38702

Missouri

Amer
P.O. Box 16551
Clayton, Missouri 63105

An organization for individuals experiencing religious discrimination and those wanting information on the occult.

Nevada

Twisted Rose Branches
5545 Mission Road
Fallon, Nevada 89406

A regional referral network for like-minded Pagans. For more information, contact Lady Bronwyn.

New Hampshire

Aura Pro Nobis
P.O. Box 178
Stratham, New Hampshire 03885

A national networking and support group for Pagans. Provides police and religious harassment contacts and occasionally puts out a newsletter.

Ordo Mysterium Baphe-Metis, Inc.
P.O. Box 156
West Nottingham, New Hampshire 03291
(603) 942-7474

A religious, philosophical, and educational organization for the Thelemic and occult communities.

New York

The American Society for Psychical Research, Inc.
5 W. 73rd Street
New York, New York 10023

The purpose and scope of the society is to investigate all forms of paranormal and psychic phenomena; to collect, classify, study, and publish such reports; and to maintain a library on psychical research and other related subjects. It publishes a journal and newsletter. Write for membership and subscription information.

Coven Mandragora
c/o North Country Wicca
P.O. Box 264
Bombay, New York 12914

A magickal circle of friends devoted to the ancient occult arts, healing, Sabbat observances, and the worship of both the Goddess and the Horned God. The group's main tradition is Eclectic Wicca, and our covenstead lies beyond the Adirondacks in northern Franklin County, New York, near the Canadian border. All who seek a positive path are welcome—women, men, straight, gay, or trans-gendered. For correspondence or information, send a self-addressed stamped envelope.

New Moon, New York
P.O. Box 1471
Madison Square Station
New York, New York 10159
(212) 662-1080

A local nonprofit organization providing monthly workshops, public rituals, and various networking and social activities for Pagans. Publisher of the monthly newsletter *Our Pagan Times.*

North Country Wicca
P.O. Box 264
Bombay, New York 12914

A networking and spiritual organization dedicated to Goddess studies, Earth religion, healing, and all forms of positive magick. Offers psychic counseling, divinations by Tarot, Neo-Pagan and Wiccan contacts, paranormal investigating, nationwide penpal services, and correspondence courses on the Old Religion and candle crafting. At the present time it is in the process of putting together a Witchcraft museum and library to help preserve heathen heritage and enlighten the public. For more information or to donate books or occult artifacts, please write to the above address.

The Pagan Poets Society (PPS)
c/o North Country Wicca
P.O. Box 264
Bombay, New York 12914

The Pagan Poets Society is a distinguished literary circle for Pagan bards, minstrels, poets, lyricists, and verse makers. Members receive a free subscription to the biannual journal *Pagan Pride*, a free listing in the "P.P.S. Directory of Members," the opportunity to network with other Pagan poets from around the world, a free list of Pagan periodicals that publish poetry, and special member's discounts on books and services offered through the Golden Isis Press and their mail-order catalogue. To qualify for membership in the Pagan Poets Society you must be able to identify yourself and your poetry as Pagan or Neo-Pagan. (The term *Pagan* includes all traditions of Wicca and all forms of New Age, Nature, Goddess, and Earth Spirituality.) In addition, you must be able to meet at least one of the following three requirements: 1. You must have had at least one book (or chapbook) of poetry published; 2. You must have had at least three different poems published in three different magazines, journals, newsletters, or newspapers; or 3. You must be a publisher of at least one book of poetry or at least three poems of a Pagan nature. One-year membership: $13.00; two-year membership: $20.00; lifetime membership: $100. Sample copy of *Pagan Pride*: $5.00. (Please make all checks and money orders payable to Gerina Dunwich.) To receive a free membership application, please send a self-addressed stamped envelope.

Wise Woman Center
Susun Weed
P.O. Box 64
Woodstock, New York 12498

North Carolina

New Earth Church
P.O. Box 5461
New Bern, North Carolina 28561

Ohio

At the Gate (ATG)
Box 09506
Columbus, Ohio 43209

A.T.G. links singles interested in New Age philosophies, spirituality, ecology, peace, animal rights, and personal growth. Nationwide. Write for free information.

Pagan Community Council of Ohio
P.O. Box 02089
Columbus, Ohio 43202

A nonprofit organization that sponsors social, educational, and religious activities for Pagans in Ohio and surrounding areas. Sponsor of the annual Shadowmas Festival.

What's Brewing Network
P.O. Box 24067
Cincinnati, Ohio 45224

A national correspondence network for the magickal-Pagan community. Provides an information exchange and networking. It is sponsored by the programmers of a *The Witching Hour* radio broadcast, which airs on station WAIF (88.3 FM). For more information, contact Logan and Brigid.

Oklahoma

The Center for Pagan Studies
P.O. Box 4803
Tulsa, Oklahoma 74159

A nonprofit corporation dedicated to public education about Earth-based religions and associated subjects.

Gay and Lesbian Pagan Coalition (GLPC)
P.O. Box 26442
Oklahoma City, Oklahoma 73126

An international referral network for gay and lesbian Pagans (including bisexual, transgendered, and transsexual persons.) Publisher of

Festive Circles Update newsletter. For more information, contact Desmond Stone.

Oregon

The Nine Houses of Gaia, Inc.
P.O. Box 14415
Portland, Oregon 97214

A nonprofit organization and regional referral network that sponsors the Northwest Fall Equinox Festival. It also operates the Pagan Information Line and publishes a Pagan newsletter, *Open Ways.*

Veterans for Religious Freedom
National Headquarters
P.O. Box 2272
Portland, Oregon 97208

A national referral council and veterans service organization listed with the Veteran's Affairs Office in Washington, D.C. Pagan veterans who have been the victims of religious discrimination should contact this organization.

Pennsylvania

International Society for Celtic Awareness (ISCA)
P.O. Box 141
Willow Grove, Pennsylvania 19090

An international network providing educational, spiritual, and referral services to those who follow a Celtic or Druidic path. It is affiliated with Kindred Spirit, which provides educational and spiritual workshops, open Sabbats, and drumming circles. Also offers a resource guide and directory to its members for various networking contacts. For more information, contact Gofannon Moondragon.

Mother Spirit
Nan Conner, coordinator
P.O. Box 1360
Exton, Pennsylvania 19341

Pittsburgh Pagan Alliance
P.O. Box 624
Monroeville, Pennsylvania 15146

Created in 1986, its goal is to "unify the diverse occult paths in the Pittsburgh area for mutual exchanges, learning and fellowship." It is also "a clearinghouse for news, information, and exchanges of scholarly, practical, and experimental knowledge." Membership is open to all who follow a positive occult path, including the Old Religion, Wicca, Asatru, Shamanism, Druidism, Thelema, Ceremonial Magick, and Neo-Paganism. Write for more information.

The Society of Mystics Network (SOM)
P.O. Box 294
Dallastown, Pennsylvania 17313

An international network providing contacts and referrals to like-minded individuals and groups. For more information contact Iscara.

Wiccan/Pagan Press Alliance (WPPA)
Silver Ravenwolf, editor
P.O. Box 1392
Mechanicsburg, Pennsylvania 17055

Networking, Pagan publishing, and home of the Witches' Anti-Discrimination League (WADL). Publishes *Midnight Drive* newsletter.

Witches Today
P.O. Box 221
Levittown, Pennsylvania 19059

Provides networking and services for Wiccans who have experienced discrimination and those who seek more information about the Craft. For additional information, contact Tammie Jesberger.

Rhode Island

Magi
c/o Metagion
184 Angell Street
Providence, Rhode Island 02906

Magickally-associated group and information exchange.

Tennessee

Cerridwynn's Own/Pagans with Exceptionalities (COPE)
P.O. Box 4055
Bristol, Tennessee 37620

An international referral network and "phone tree" providing information and services to disabled Pagans

Southern Wiccan Council
P.O. Box 18999
Memphis, Tennessee 38181

A regional Pagan council that provides networking and contact with Pagan groups from various traditions

Texas

Ancient Arts Association
P.O. Box 6051
Fort Hood, Texas 76544

A local referral network created especially for Pagans who serve in the military.

Council of the Magickal Arts/Our Lady of the Sacred Flame
P.O. Box 33274
Austin, Texas 78764

A regional (Texas and Oklahoma) council of Pagans and Witches that organizes gatherings and publishes a journal devoted to the arts of magick. One-year membership: $15.00.

New Age Metaphysical Research Association
1201 Lake Air
Waco, Texas 76710

Nexus International
P.O. Box 532256
Dallas, Texas 75053

Networking for Pagans, Wiccans, and magickal folks.

Pagan Alliance of Central Texas (PACT)
P.O. Box 12041
Austin, Texas 78711

A regional referral network that provides education to the public and sponsors eight potlucks or informal workshops each year.

The Psychic Society
P.O. Box 331058
Fort Worth, Texas 76163

"Devoted to the research of psychic phenomena and to learning the mysteries of life." Write for its free newsletter and a membership application.

Vermont

Great Mother's Love Network
P.O. Box 8456
Burlington, Vermont 05402
(802) 862-8246

An international referral and "phone tree" created for the purpose of providing Pagan connections.

Washington

Aquarian Tabernacle Church
P.O. Box 409
Index, Washington 98256
(206) 527-2426

Founded in 1979, this group holds monthly meetings, sponsors festivals, and provides various services to the Pagan and Wiccan community, including a twenty-four-hour recorded events line: (206) LA-PAGAN.

Dionysia
P.O. Box 30511
Seattle, Washington 98103
(206) 322-8572

Pagan Family Alliance (PFA)
P.O. Box 30806
Greenwich Station
Seattle, Washington 98103

A networking and information group founded by Pagan-identified parents who want to know what similar parents are doing to foster their children's spiritual growth. Their goal is to publish educational materials for parents. Write for additional information or to send your input.

Wisconsin

Circle Sanctuary
P.O. Box 219
Mount Horeb, Wisconsin 53572
(608) 924-2216

A legally-recognized Shamanic Wiccan Church and nonprofit multicultural Nature and spirituality resource center, founded in 1974. It provides international networking, workshops, training programs, and ministerial services, and publishes *Circle Network News, Circle Guide to Pagan Groups, Pagan Spirit Alliance Newsletter and Directory, Sanctuary Circles,* and *Circle Network Bulletin.* Circle also sponsors the annual Pagan Spirit Gathering and a variety of other festivals, retreats, and events. For more information, write or call weekdays between 1 P.M. and 4 P.M. (Central Standard Time.)

The Earth Conclave
P.O. Box 14377
Madison, Wisconsin 53714

An eco-spiritual and educational organization focusing on environmental issues. Holds meetings eight times throughout the year.

Lady Liberty League
c/o Circle
P.O. Box 219
Mount Horeb, Wisconsin 53572
(608) 924-2216; Fax: (608) 924-5961

A referral network of volunteers affiliated with Circle Network and dedicated to assisting Wiccans, Pagans, and Nature Spiritualists with religious freedom cases. Contact them if you have news to report or if you are interested in being a part of the league.

Occulterian Life Church of Wicca

P.O. Box K
Athens, Wisconsin 54411
(715) 257-7195

Founded in 1993 by Apophis Valkyrie, this tradition advocates communing with nature with little emphasis on deity identities, but perceives the Divine Union as a whole. Other branch organizations incorporated with this church are the Solitary Pagan Alliance and the Alternative Religions Alliance. Its ministry is a diverse group that includes Wiccans, Pagans, and others on the polytheistic level. Future projects include *Webweaver*, an international Pagan and Wiccan newsletter.

Of a Like Mind Network (OALM)

P.O. Box 6677
Madison, Wisconsin 53716

An international referral network providing its members with a networking services guide, access to a support hotline, local contacts for spiritual women, and free announcements and ads in its newspaper. To become a member, a subscription to *Of a Like Mind* and a $5.00 fee are required.

Pagan Spirit Alliance (PSA)

c/o Circle
P.O. Box 219
Mount Horeb, Wisconsin 53572

This is "a special Pagan friendship network within Circle Network." It is made up of Pagan individuals who are attuned to positive (helping and healing) magickal ways. One-year membership is a donation of $25.00 or more (U.S. and Canada, $30.00 elsewhere). Members receive a listing in and copy of the P.S.A. membership directory, a subscription to the quarterly P.S.A. newsletter, discounts on certain seminars, workshops, and the festival registration fee for the International Pagan Spirit Gathering, held each summer, and admission to P.S.A. members' meetings.

Reformed Congregation of the Goddess
P.O. Box 6677
Madison, Wisconsin 53716
(608) 244-0072

A Dianic Wiccan group founded in 1983. It sponsors monthly worship services, workshops and conferences for feminist women, and publishes a newspaper that focuses on women's spirituality.

Canada

CERES
Site L, Box 21
RR 1, Kispiox Road
Hazelton, British Columbia V0J 1Y0
Canada

Pagans for Peace Network
P.O. Box 2205
Clearbrook, British Columbia V2T 3X8
Canada

An international referral network providing a newsletter and contacts for politically-active left-wing Pagans and Wiccans. For additional information, contact Samuel Wagar.

The Wiccan Church of Canada
109 Vaughan Road
Toronto, Ontario M6C 2L9
Canada

The Wiccan Information Network
P.O. Box 2422
Main Post Office
Vancouver, British Columbia V6B 3W7
Canada

United Kingdom

London Druid Group
Gordon Gentry
74 Riversmeet
Hertford SG14 1LE
England

The Order of Bards, Ovates, and Druids
P.O. Box 1333
Lewes, East Sussex BN7 3ZG
England
Founded in 1717, this group (Druid Tradition) holds monthly meetings, has over one thousand members around the world, and provides a "postal experience-based training program." For more information, contact Philip Carr-Gomm.

Pagans Against Nukes (PAN)
Blaenberem, Mynyddcerrig
Llanelli, Dyfed County
Wales SA15 5BL
United Kingdom

The Pagan Federation
Box BM 7097
London WC1N 3XX
England
Founded in 1971, this is one of Europe's oldest Pagan organizations. It works to educate the public, media, and authorities about Pagan values, beliefs, and practices, and to defend Paganism against misrepresentation. It promotes interaction between Pagans through its contact and pen pal networks and its excellent forty-page quarterly magazine, *Pagan Dawn.*

The Society for Psychical Research
49 Marloes Road
London W8 6LA
England
Phone: 071-937-8984

Founded in 1882, its "purpose is to examine without prejudice or prepossession and in a scientific spirit those faculties of man, real or supposed, which appear to be inexplicable on any generally recognized hypothesis." It publishes a quarterly journal (one-year subscription: $36.00/£ 20) that focuses on all forms of paranormal phenomena. Address all membership inquiries to the secretary at the above address.

Australia

Church of All Worlds
Australian Headquarters
P.O. Box 408, Woden, ACT
Australia 2606
Phone: 06-299-2432; fax: 06-299-4100

Order of the Silver Star
P.O. Box 570
Parkes, New South Wales
Australia 2870

A religious organization involved with Hermetic Magick.

France

Wicca International Witchcraft
6 rue Danton
94270 Kremlin-Bicetre
France

Germany

B. Norris Perry, MHR
6412-B Hurtgen Drive
Anderson Barracks
D-55278 Dexheim, Germany
Phone: 049-6133-60323

Solitary Wiccan (member no. P5149792 of the American Counseling Association) offers FREE counseling services to depressed or troubled sisters and brothers in the Pagan community. Confidential therapy. (Also member of the Association for Specialists in Group Work; the International Association for Addictions and Offender Counselors.)

Japan

Japanese Pagan Network
Ikari Segawa
7-22-4 Minamisyowa-Cho
Tokushima City 770
Japan

2

PAGAN AND WICCAN CHURCHES

In this section you will find a state-by-state directory of legally-recognized Wiccan and Pagan churches and related organizations throughout the United States (and one in Canada). Other churches, covens, and spiritual groups can be found in the first section, "Organizations."

Arizona

The Divine Circle of the Sacred Grove   16845 N. 29th Avenue, no. 1346, Phoenix, Arizona 85023; (602) 230-4186

New Age Community Church   6418 S. 39th Avenue, Phoenix, Arizona 85041; (602) 237-3213

Ring of Troth, Inc.   P.O. Box 25637, Tempe, Arizona 85285

California

Ancient Keltic Church   P.O. Box 663, Tujunga, California, 91043

Celtic Witan Church   21000 Lull Street, Canoga Park, California 91304

Church of All Worlds   P.O. Box 1542, Ukiah, California 95483; (510) 549-7777

Covenant of the Goddess   P.O. Box 1226, Berkeley, California 94701

Fellowship of the Spiral Path   P.O. Box 5521, Berkeley, California 94705

Reclaiming Collective   P.O. Box 14404, San Francisco, California 94114; (510) 236-4645

Connecticut

Fanscifiaroan   106 Center Street, Southington, Connecticut 06489; (203) 621-3579

Moonshadow Institute of the Old Religion   P.O. Box 119, Oneco, Connecticut 06373; (401) 397-8857

Florida

The Church of Iron Oak   P.O. Box 060672, Palm Bay, Florida 32906; (407) 722-0291

Labyrinth Temple of the Goddess   615 W. Virginia, Tampa, Florida 33603; (813) 224-0274

Wiccan Religious Cooperative of Florida, Inc.   3936 S. Semoran Boulevard, Suite 116, Orlando, Florida 32822; (407) 657-2182; (407) 725-4316

Georgia

Keltic Orthodox Order of the Royal Oak P.O. Box 6006, Athens, Georgia 30604; (706) 369-6813

Illinois

Circle of Danu c/o B. Dering, 1310 W. Lunt Avenue, Apt. 507, Chicago, Illinois 60640; (312) 262-0203

First Temple of the Craft of WICA P.O. Box 59, Western Springs, Illinois 60558

Panthea Unitarian Universalist Pagan Fellowship P.O. Box 608031, Chicago, Illinois 60660; (708) 492-1642

Maryland

Free Spirit Alliance P.O. Box 25242, Baltimore, Maryland 21229; (301) 604-6049

Free Spirit Alliance P.O. Box 5358, Laurel, Maryland 20726; (301) 604-6049

Massachusetts

Earthspirit P.O. Box 365, Medford, Massachusetts 02155; (617) 395-1023; Fax: (617) 396-5066

The Iseum of Venus Healing (The Church of Isis Rising) P.O. Box 698, Ayer, Massachusetts 01432

Michigan

The Religious Order of the Sons of Heimdallr P.O. Box 814, Douglas, Michigan 49406; (616) 857-4463

Sanctuary of the Silver Moon P.O. Box 6052, Grand Rapids, Michigan 49516

Missouri

Greenleaf Coven P.O. Box 924, Springfield, Missouri 65802; (417) 865-5903

Sanctuary of Formative Spirituality P.O. Box 159, Salem, Missouri 65560; (314) 689-2400

New Hampshire

Our Lady of Enchantment 39 Amherst Street, Nashua, New Hampshire 03060; (603) 880-7237

New Mexico

The Church of Our Lady of the Woods, Inc. P.O. Box 1107, Los Alamos, New Mexico 87544; (505) 662-5333

Our Lady of the Shining Staar P.O. Box 520, Church Rock, New Mexico 87311; (505) 488-5364

New York

Ar nDraiocht Fein: A Druid Fellowship, Inc. P.O. Box 516, East Syracuse, New York 13057; (800) DRUIDRY

Hawthorn Grove, Inc. P.O. Box 706, Monticello, New York 12701

Temple of Eternal Light 928 E. 5th Street, Brooklyn, New York 11230; (718) 438-4878

Ohio

Association of Earth Religion Churches P.O. Box 141358, Columbus, Ohio 43214; (614) 263-7611

Church of Earth Healing 22 Palmer Street, Athens, Ohio 45701; (614) 592-6193

Green Dome Temple 1791 Westwood Avenue, Cincinnati, Ohio 45214

Temple of Wicca P.O. Box 2281, Lancaster, Ohio 43130

Rhode Island

The Society of the Evening Star, Inc. P.O. Box 29182, Providence, Rhode Island 02909; (401) 273-1176

Utah

Moonspun Circle 1603 South 1200E, Salt Lake City, Utah 84105; (801) 467-3780

Vermont

Church of the Sacred Earth: A Union of Pagan Congregations RR 1, Box 239, Christian Hill Road, Bethal, Vermont 05032; (802) 234-9670

Washington

Aquarian Tabernacle Church P.O. Box 409, Index, Washington 98256; (206) 793-1945

Rowan Tree Church 9724 132 Avenue NE, Kirkland, Washington 98033

West Virginia

Free Association of Lillians P.O. Box 890, Morgantown, West Virginia 26505; (304) 296-3008; fax: (304) 296-3311

Wisconsin

Circle Sanctuary P.O. Box 219, Mount Horeb, Wisconsin 53572; (608) 924-2216; fax: (608) 924-5961

Re-Formed Congregation of the Goddess P.O. Box 6677, Madison, Wisconsin 53716; (608) 244-0072

Spiritpath P.O. Box 236, Gays Mills, Wisconsin 54631; (608) 735-4720

Canada

Congregationalist Witchcraft Association P.O. Box 2205, Clearbrook, British Columbia V2T 3X8, Canada

3

SCHOOLS

"Knowledge is power."

—BACON

The following list includes many schools that offer courses on Wicca, the magickal arts, natural healing, Voodoo and herbalism, just to name a few. Most teach through correspondence courses; however, there are quite a few that offer public classes and even individual training to the serious seeker of knowledge.

Alaska

The Denali Institute of Northern Traditions
P.O. Box 671510
Chugiak, Alaska 99567

Offers lessons by mail in the Northern Spiritual Tradition, as well as a Rune Master program.

Arizona

The Divine Circle of the Sacred Grove
16845 N. 29th Avenue, no. 1346
Phoenix, Arizona 85023
(602) 230-4186

This committed order of Druids and Wiccans offers instruction by both correspondence and through seminars on the Religion of the Old Ways. (They also perform legal handfastings and other rites of passage.)

Wicca, An Introduction Taught by Rik Johnson
c/o Desert Henge Coven
P.O. Box 40451
Tucson, Arizona 85717
(520) 323-8112

"Explore the mystery, magick, and beauty of Wicca (Witchcraft). Despite common misconceptions, Wicca is a joyous, life-loving nature religion that honors the God and Goddess, and encourages personal growth and living in harmony with the Earth. Held yearly since 1982, this is Arizona's oldest public class on Wicca. It emphasizes the traditional beliefs and practices of Wicca and explores the history, mythology, magick, and rituals of Wicca. The class uses slides, lectures, music, displays, handouts, and discussions to further illustrate the subject."

California

Church of All Worlds
c/o Tony Navarro
Central Nest Liaison
P.O. Box 1542
Ukiah, California 95482
(415) 585-8228

This group, founded in 1962, offers classes on the following subjects: dance, healing, herbcraft, magick, massage, music, nature religions, and psychic development. Training for ordination into the Church of All Worlds priesthood is also available.

Circle of Aradia
P.O. Box 1608
Topanga, California 90290

This group sponsors classes and one-day workshops for women only on Feminist Witchcraft and Dianic Wicca.

The Hermetic Order of the Eternal Golden Dawn
14050 Cherry Avenue, Suite R-159
Fontana, California 92337

A mystery school and fraternity that teaches the mysteries of Hermetics, Qabala, Tarot, healing, ceremonial magick, Mystical Christianity, meditation, astral projection, Neo-Paganism, inner alchemy and self-mastery. Members receive personalized instruction, temple work, and an opportunity to learn and share the Western Mystery Tradition with other like-minded people in a friendly atmosphere. To hear their brief taped message, call (909) 341-5628 or (310) 289-7214.

Metaphysics College
P.O. Box 728
Glendora, California 91740

Offers metaphysics and psychology courses. Write for a free brochure.

Priesthood
2301 Artesia Boulevard, Suite 12-188
Redondo Beach, California 90278
(310) 397-1310

It offers "a complete and advanced metaphysical, magickal and psychic power development correspondence course." Students can expect methods that are simple to understand and easy to apply. Write or call for a free brochure and rates.

Reclaiming Collective
P.O. Box 14404
San Francisco, California 94114
Events Line: (510) 236-4645

This is a group that belongs to the American Neo-Witchcraft tradition called the Reclaiming Tradition. Write for more information regarding its classes, workshops, and retreats.

Shadowlight Institute
1965 Prince Albert Drive
Riverside, California 92507

It offers courses in Medicine Path, metaphysics, healing, and much more. For more information and a catalog listing descriptions of their courses, faculty, certification opportunities, and methods of individual education design, send a check or money order in the amount of $2.00 to Shadowlight Products, Inc.

University of Egyptian Arts
P.O. Box 90062
San Diego, California 92109

Its home study course "now makes available much previously esoteric material." Send $1.00 for a detailed brochure and catalog.

Colorado

Fortress Temple
P.O. Box 172271
Denver, Colorado 80217
(303) 399-2971

A Wiccan-oriented group that offers weekly classes. Special training is offered to children (from ages five to twelve) of Pagan adults by their Education for Pagan Youth Committee.

Yero Wolo Spiritual Circle
3000 East Colfax, no. 355
Denver, Colorado 80206
(303) 754-2994

This group, founded on the "principles of traditional African spirituality," offers classes, workshops, and correspondence of "Neo-African spiritual practices."

Florida

As Always Coven
2568 E. Fowler Avenue
Tampa, Florida 33612
(813) 972-1766

Write or call for information regarding its one-year class in Wicca.

Church of the Seven African Powers
P.O. Box 453336
Miami, Florida 33245

Write for free information on its correspondence course and initiations. "Learn how to work with the gods and goddesses of West Africa to improve your life materially and spiritually."

Circle of the Moonlit Sea
649 S.W. Whitmore Drive
Port St. Lucie, Florida 34984
(407) 879-0578

This is a British-Traditional group that offers several eight-week introductory courses in Wicca throughout the year.

Wiccan Religious Cooperative of Florida, Inc.
3936 S. Semoran Boulevard, Suite 116
Orlando, Florida 32822
(407) 725-4316; (407) 657-2182

Write or call for more information about their educational classes, workshops, seminars, and other activities.

Georgia

Bangor Institute
P.O. Box 4196
Athens, Georgia 30605

Write for more information about the classes offered by this holistic college.

Knight of Runes
P.O. Box 2070
Decatur, Georgia 30031

A home study course in powerful rune magick, taught by a European rune master.

Indiana

Circle of Isis Rising
Elkhart Branch, Indiana
(219) 262-3483

A multi-traditional fellowship and Hermetic lodge offering classes on the following subjects: divination, magick, metaphysics, psychic development, and Wicca. Also offers counseling services. Call for more information.

Illinois

The Iseum of the Goddess of the Crystal Moon
P.O. Box 802
Matteson, Illinois 60443

Internationally recognized as an Iseum with the Fellowship of Isis (from Ireland), this group offers courses in Wicca through both classroom instruction and correspondence.

Temple of Kriya Yoga
2414 N. Kedzie Avenue
Chicago, Illinois 60647
(800) 248-0024

A center of spiritual study offering a wide selection of publications, audio- and videotapes, classes, and seminars. Professional astrology course, Tarot, palmistry, the mysteries of ancient Egypt, astral projection, and more. Accepts Visa and Mastercard. Call or write for a free catalog.

Massachusetts

Full Circle
37 Clark Road
Cummington, Massachusetts 01026
(413) 634-0262

This is a center for spiritual and community development that offers both public and private instruction and various workshops in areas such as sacred mask-making, meditation, exploring the Goddess within and among us, and the Wheel of the Year.

Michigan

Goddess Studies
1402 Hill Street
Ann Arbor, Michigan 48104
(313) 665-5550

An eclectic Wiccan group that provides public classes. For more information, contact Aurora.

New Hampshire

Our Lady of Enchantment
P.O. Box 1366
Nashua, New Hampshire 03061
(603) 880-7237

Five complete home study courses are available: Witchcraft, Sorcery, Egyptian Ritual Magick, Herbology, and Divination. Also offer on-campus training in the magickal arts at their metaphysical center in Nashua, New Hampshire. Open daily to all sincere seekers. Call or write for a free information package.

New Mexico

Our Lady of the Woods
P.O. Box 1107
Los Alamos, New Mexico 87544
(505) 662-5333

A British- and Celtic-oriented Wiccan coven that sponsors weekly classes in divination, magick, and other areas. Membership is open to all, regardless of race or sexual orientation.

New York

Lodge Uraeus/Servants of the Light
P.O. Box 4538
Sunnyside, New York 11104

For information regarding its course, Servants of the Light, send a self-addressed stamped envelope.

Temple of the Eternal Light
  928 E. Fifth Street
  Brooklyn, New York 11230
  (718) 438-4878

This Wicca/Ceremonial Magick/Qabalah-oriented group offers individual and group workshops and home study programs in "Thirteen Tools Towards Enlightenment," Qabalah, ceremonial magick, and Wicca.

The Wheel of Wisdom School
  c/o Gerina Dunwich
  P.O. Box 525
  Fort Covington, New York 12937

Eight lessons by mail, taught by Gerina Dunwich, a well-known Witch and Wiccan book author. Each lesson corresponds to one of the eight Sabbats celebrated throughout the course of the year and teaches the meaning of that particular Sabbat, along with its sacred herbs, gemstones, and Pagan deities. With each lesson the student also receives altar-decorating suggestions, directions for making Sabbat potpourri, and a Sabbat ritual designed for either Solitary Witches or covens (students should specify their preference when enrolling). Four different courses are available: The Complete Wheel (all eight Sabbats): $35.00; The Greater Sabbats (four lessons): $18.00; The Lesser Sabbats (four lessons): $18.00; or One Lesson (student must specify which Sabbat): $5.00. Please make checks and money orders payable to Gerina Dunwich (U.S. funds only).

North Carolina

The School of Wicca
  P.O. Box 1502
  New Bern, North Carolina 28563

It offers courses in Celtic Witchcraft, practical sorcery, Tantra, Yoga, prediction, astral travel, astrology, healing, and a complete course on mystical awareness.

Stardust Circle
  Seminary Admissions Office
  P.O. Box 2474
  Durham, North Carolina 27715

  If offers a correspondence course that is "divided into five afford-able units of six lessons each on cassette tape." For more information, send a long self-addressed stamped envelope.

Ohio

The Center
  P.O. Box 104
  Sylvania, Ohio 43560

  A Shaman-apprentice program with Owl Woman. Write for more information regarding its one-year guided cross-cultural program.

Church of Universal Forces
  P.O. Box 03195
  Columbus, Ohio 43203
  (614) 252-2083

  It offers a correspondence course in Wicca and Voodoo. Write or call for more information.

Texas

School of Woodland Celtic Wicca
  c/o C. R. Fagan
  3114 Jubilee Trail
  Austin, Texas 78748

  A Celtic Wiccan group that offers standard coven training and Book of Shadows by correspondence to all who pledge to abide by the Wiccan Rede.

Virginia

The International Academy of Hermetic Knowledge
  2150 Wise Street
  P.O. Box 4384
  Charlottesville, Virginia 22905

"A Qabalistic, Gnostic, Egyptian Magickal Organization," a function of the Holy Order of the Winged Disc. Write for more information.

Washington

The Hermit's Grove
9724 132nd Avenue N.E.
Kirkland, Washington 98033
(206) 828-4124

A nonprofit educational center offering on-site classes, workshops, a Stone Circle for meditation and solitude, and facilities for student research. It is associated with the Rowan Tree Church and also offers a home study course. Classes average $10.00 to $15.00 per class. Workstudy and barter are also available. Write for more information.

School of the Seasons
1463 E. Republican, no. 187
Seattle, Washington 98112

A correspondence course based on the idea of working with seasonal energies and metaphors. Packets available for each season suggesting tasks and readings in natural studies, personal growth, magickal skills, seasonal celebrations, festival foods, sacred crafts, and Goddess lore. Instructor Waverly Fitzgerald edits *The Beltane Papers: A Journal of Women's Mysteries* and studied with Starhawk. Send a self-addressed stamped envelope for information.

Uranus Publishing Company, Inc.
401 Pond Lane
Sequim, Washington 98382

Write for free information about its correspondence courses on astrology: Ove H. Sehested's Master Course in Basic Astrology and the Self-Teach Course.

Wisconsin

Circle
P.O. Box 219
Mount Horeb, Wisconsin 53572
(608) 924-2216

Circle Sanctuary is a Shamanic Wiccan church and multicultural Nature Spirituality resource center that offers education and training programs. For more information, write or call weekdays between the hours of 1 P.M. and 4 P.M. (Central Standard Time.)

United Kingdom

The Institute for Progressive and Scientific Occultism
Attention: P. Cooper
16 Aynho Crescent
Sunnyside, Northampton NN2 8JY
England

It offers a home study course, with the advantage of personal tuition, that starts through a series of graduated exercises from the first principles to a full understanding of the science of magick. The course includes instruction in constructing the "Cosmic Inworld," dealing with symbols, the four elements, the planets, the cosmic tides, and more. There are no books to buy and payment can be spread out over a period of time at no extra cost.

Vivianne Crowley
BM DEOSIL
London WC1N 3XX
England

British coven elders offer correspondence training for newcomers to the Craft. Send $4.00 for more information or $20.00 for Part One.

New Zealand

The Australasian College of Herbal Studies
P.O. Box 35146
Browns Bay, Auckland
New Zealand
Phone: 64-9-473-5573

United States office:
P.O. Box 57
Lake Oswego, Oregon 97034

(503) 635-6652; fax: (503) 697-0615; voice mail:
(800) 48-STUDY

At the present time they offer eleven home study courses in natural healing. To receive a prospectus that outlines the courses, or if you need additional information, please call, write, or send e-mail.

4

Books and Publishers

"A good book is the precious life-blood of a master spirit,
embalmed and treasured up on purpose to a life
beyond life."

—MILTON

The companies listed below publish and sell New Age and Wicca books. Whether you are looking for a good book to read or are writing one yourself, chances are you will find exactly what you're looking for within the following pages. (Additional book dealers can be located in Section 8, "Magickal and Metaphysical Shops," and in Section 9, "Mail Order."

Most of the publishers listed here are the major companies that deal with the subjects of Witchcraft, the New Age, psychic sciences, and the magickal arts. If you are considering writing such a book or have already written one and are in search of a publisher, you will find many to choose from.

Included in each publisher's listing are the types of books published along with basic guidelines for manuscript submissions. Even if not specified in the listing, it is always a good practice to include a self-addressed stamped envelope with adequate return postage whenever submitting a manuscript, outline, or query letter. If you are writing to a publisher outside of the United States, be sure to include the proper amount of international reply coupons (IRC's), which can be obtained at just about any U.S. post office. (Many publishing companies will not answer a query letter or return a rejected manuscript unless a self-addressed stamped envelope or return envelope with IRC's is provided.)

For more information about writing books and the publishing business, I recommend that you read a current edition of *Writer's Market* magazine.

Alexandria Books

1342 Naglee Avenue
San Jose, California 95191
(800) 241-5422

Call or write for a free catalog of metaphysical and mystical books.

Aquarian Press

77–85 Fulham Palace Road
Hammersmith, London W68JB
England
Fax: 081-307-4440

Publishes books (approximately fifty to sixty titles per year) on astrology, the divinatory arts, the New Age, psychic awareness, spirituality, and other subjects. Writers outside of England are advised to query first with a self-addressed envelope and international reply coupons (IRC's), which can be obtained at their local post offices. Free book catalog available on request.

Aradia Books

P.O. Box 972-G
Burlington, Vermont 05402

Women's spirituality, priestess craft, Goddess studies, Earth religion, positive magick, and other topics. Catalog: $1.00.

Astro Communications Services (ACS Publications)
P.O. Box 34487
San Diego, California 92163

Publisher of astrology books. Writers are advised to query first. To receive their free book catalog or manuscript guidelines, send a 9″ × 12″ self-addressed envelope along with two first-class stamps.

Bear and Co., Inc.
P.O. Box 2860
Santa Fe, New Mexico 87504
(505) 983-9868

A spiritually-oriented publishing company interested in books on the New Age, Western mystics, ecology, and those that "heal and celebrate the Earth." Writers are advised to query first or submit an outline along with several sample chapters. To receive a free catalog, send a 9″ × 12″ self-addressed envelope along with three first-class stamps.

Bill's Books
150 E. Whitestone Boulevard
Cedar Park, Texas 78613

Rare books on metaphysics, alchemy, Freemasonry, Witchcraft, Qabalah, and other topics. "Top dollar paid for used occult books." Catalog: $1.00.

Blue Dolphin Publishing, Inc.
P.O. Box 1908
Nevada City, California 95959
(916) 265-6925; fax: (916) 265-0787

Publisher of "comparative spiritual traditions" and books for individuals interested in self-growth and planetary awareness. Writers are advised to submit an outline along with sample chapters and a self-addressed stamped envelope. Free book catalog available upon request.

Carol Publishing Group/Citadel Press
120 Enterprise Avenue
Secaucus, New Jersey 07094
(800) 447-BOOK

"For over thirty years, the Citadel Library of the Mystic Arts has been hailed as America's definitive line of works on occult sciences and personalities, magick, demonology, spiritualism, mysticism, natural health, psychic sciences, Witchcraft, metaphysics, and esoterica." Writers are advised to submit an outline or synopsis along with several sample chapters. Call or write for a free book catalog.

Cassandra Press
P.O. Box 868
San Rafael, California 94915
(415) 382-8507; fax: (415) 382-7758

Publisher of New Age, holistic health, and metaphysical books. Writers are advised to submit an outline along with sample chapters. Free book catalog and manuscript guidelines available upon request.

Delphi Press, Inc.
P.O. Box 267990
Chicago, Illinois 60626
(312) 274-791; fax: (312) 274-7912

Publishes books about divination, healing, magick, Nature and Earth religions, Paganism, Wicca, Witchcraft, women's spirituality, and men's mysteries. Also publishes poetry. Writers are advised to submit complete manuscript or an outline along with three sample chapters. Free book catalog and manuscript guidelines available upon request.

E. J. M. Publishing, Inc.
976 Murfreesboro Road
Nashville, Tennessee 37217
(615) 781-8835

A small press that publishes books dealing with the paranormal and eyewitness accounts of UFO sightings.

Hampton Roads Publishing Company, Inc.
976 Norfolk Square
Norfolk, Virginia 23502
(804) 459-2453; fax: (804) 455-8907

Publishes New Age books and occult fiction, among other subjects. Writers are advised to first submit a proposal and outline. To receive a free catalog, send a 9" × 12" self-addressed envelope along with two first-class stamps.

Harper San Francisco
Division of HarperCollins
1160 Battery Street, 3rd Floor
San Francisco, California 94111
(415) 477-4400; fax: (415) 477-4444

Publishes books about new consciousness, spirituality, theology, and women's issues and studies, among other subjects. Writers are advised to query first or submit an outline along with sample chapters. Free catalog and manuscript guidelines available upon request.

Hay House, Inc.
P.O. Box 6204
Carson, California 90749
(310) 605-0601

Among the various subjects published are New Age and philosophy, and books with "a positive self-help/metaphysical slant." Writers are advised to query first or submit an outline along with sample chapters. Free catalog upon request.

Humanics Publishing Group
1482 Mecaslin Street N.W.
Atlanta, Georgia 30309
fax: (404) 874-1976

Publishes New Age books in addition to other subjects. Writers are advised to submit an outline with at least three sample chapters. Send a self-addressed stamped envelope for a free catalog or manuscript guidelines.

In Print Publishing
65 Verde Valley School Road, Suite F-2
Sedona, Arizona 86336
(602) 284-1370

A small press publisher with an interest in metaphysical how-to books.

Inner Traditions, International
One Park Street
Rochester, Vermont 05767
(802) 767-3174; fax: (802) 767-3726

"For the past twenty years, Inner Traditions has been a leading publisher of quality books on alternative health and spirituality, metaphysics, and indigenous cultures of the world." Also publishes books on mythology, the New Age, esoteric philosophy, and women's issues and studies. Writers are advised to query first or submit an outline along with several sample chapters and a self-addressed stamped envelope. Free book catalog and guidelines available upon request.

Llewellyn Publications
P.O. Box 64383
St. Paul, Minnesota 55164
(612) 291-1970; fax: (612) 291-1908

Publishes books dealing with the divinatory arts, alternative health, applied magick, herbs, metaphysics, Wicca-as-religion, Shamanic techniques, the occult, Paganism, Witchcraft, the New Age, and women's issues and studies. Writers are advised to submit an outline along with sample chapters. Free manuscript guidelines are available. To receive a book catalog, send a 9" × 12" self-addressed envelope along with four first-class stamps.

Middle Earth Books
P.O. Box 81906
Rochester Hills, Michigan 48308
(313) 656-4989

Scarce and rare metaphysical titles. Catalog: $3.00.

New Horizons Press
11659 Doverwood Drive
Riverside, California 92505

A small-press publishing house that specializes in New Age books.

Newcastle Publishing Company, Inc.
13419 Saticoy Street
North Hollywood, California 91605
(213) 873-3191; fax: (213) 780-2007

Publishes holistic health, metaphysical, New Age, and self-help books. Writers are advised to query first or submit an outline along with sample chapters. Free book catalog. To receive manuscript guidelines, send a self-addressed stamped envelope.

Occult Bookstore
1561 N. Milwaukee Avenue
Chicago, Illinois 60622
(312) 292-0995

Specialists in metaphysics, featuring a large selection of books on all spiritual traditions. Also buys used books. Send a self-addressed stamped envelope to receive a free catalog.

Original Publications
P.O. Box 236
Old Bethpage, New York 11804

Over 450 titles on metaphysics, dreams, Witchcraft, candle burning, Tarot, divination, Santeria, and more. Catalog: $2.00.

Samuel Weiser, Inc.
P.O. Box 612
York Beach, Maine 03910
(207) 363-4393

Publishes books dealing with astrology, esoterica, the magickal arts, metaphysics, Oriental philosophy, Qabalah, Tarot, but no poetry or novels. Writers are advised to submit complete manuscript. Free catalog upon request.

Serpent's Occult Books
P.O. Box 290644
Pt. Orange, Florida 32129
(904) 760-7675

Top dollar paid for used occult books. Scarce editions offered and out-of-print titles. New and used book lists available. Write or call for a free catalog.

Sun Books
Box 5588
Santa Fe, New Mexico 87502

Publishes books on astrology, Earth changes, healing, the occult, and more. Write for a free booklist.

The Theosophical Publishing House
306 W. Geneva Road
Wheaton, Illinois 60187
(708) 665-0130; fax: (708) 665-8791

Publishes books on the following subjects: astrology, comparative religion, Eastern and Western religions, health and healing, meditation, Native American spirituality, the New Age, women's and men's spirituality, and yoga. They also accept nonfiction translations. Writers are advised to query first or submit an outline along with sample chapters. Free book catalog. Send a self-addressed stamped envelope to receive manuscript guidelines.

5

PERIODICALS

The following is an alphabetically-arranged listing of most of the magazines, newspapers, literary journals and newsletters published by and for members of the Wiccan, Pagan, or New Age communities. All efforts have been made to keep subscription rates, addresses, and editors up-to-date (though these sometimes seem to change as often as the Moon changes its phase).

Most of the periodicals listed here welcome the submission of articles, poetry, spells, ritual outlines, and artwork from freelancers. Write for guidelines (usually free if available) from the ones that interest you, and always have the courtesy of enclosing a self-addressed stamped envelope when submitting material for publication or whenever sending correspondence that requires a reply or forwarding. (If you are writing to periodicals outside of the United States, be sure to enclose a return envelope with the proper amount of international reply coupons (IRC's), which can be obtained at most U.S. post offices.

Most of the periodicals listed here offer payment to writers in the form of free contributor's copies. A few pay in cash, and some of the smaller presses cannot afford to make a payment of any kind but will publish you and give you the opportunity and pleasure of seeing your work in print and sharing it with others of a like mind.

If you are searching for Pagan pen pals, new friends, or a soul mate, this section is an ideal place to begin, for many of the periodicals contain a section for contacts, networking, and ads. Rates vary from free to inexpensive to moderately-priced.

Pagan journals and newsletters contain some of the best writing and poetry around, as well as traditional Witch recipes, information on magick and Sabbat ceremonies, reviews, announcements, and news to keep you updated on the events and changes constantly taking place throughout the Wiccan community.

Wherever your interests lie—Dianic feminist Wicca, gay spirituality, Thelema, Pagan political activism, modern Druidism, Goddess-oriented poetry, or Pagan parenting—there is a periodical somewhere here just for you.

Aamulet Newsletter
Nicole Everett, editor
P.O. Box 123
Coos Bay, Oregon 97420

A quarterly newsletter from Circle of Isis Rising. Sample copy: $2.50; one-year subscription: $10.00.

Accord
Lila Harman, editor
P.O. Box 33274
Austin, Texas 78764

A quarterly journal of the Council of the Magickal Arts (C.M.A.). Established in 1980. Sample copy: $2.50; one-year subscription: $10.00.

Acorns
Lady Amethyst, editor
P.O. Box 6006
Athens, Georgia 30604
(706) 369-6813

A quarterly magazine of Wicca and Paganism. Sample copy: $2.50; one-year subscription: $12.00.

Aerious Journal
Mark S. McNutt, editor
93640 Deadwood Creek Road
Deadwood, Oregon 97430
(503) 964-5341

A quarterly magazine of Earth and Spirit. Networking, articles, letters, reviews, and more. Sample copy: $3.00; one-year subscription: $15.00; Canadian subscription: $20.00. Back issues are available for $2.50.

Aladrisa's Cauldron
P.O. Box 132
Breslau, Ontario NOB 1NO
Canada

"A Wiccan/Pagan journal published nine times per year on the Greater Sabbats. News, articles, kid's corner, networking." Write for more information regarding sample copies and subscription rates.

Ancient Arts
P.O. Box 3127
Morgantown, West Virginia 26505
Sample copy: $4.00.

Ancient Pathways
P.O. Box 2171
Kokomo, Indiana 46904

"A newsletter exploring many spiritual paths." Sample copy: $1.00.

Ancient Religions Newsletter
Anna Nelson, editor
1157½ W. 30th Street, Box B3
Los Angeles, California 90007
(213) 856-2824

A Pagan newsletter published eight times per year. Sample copy: 50¢; back issues: 75¢; one-year subscription: $5.00, Canadian subscription: $7.00; other countries: $10.00.

Anichti Poli
Sofia Mandilas, editor
P.O. Box 20037
Athens GR-11810
Greece

A quarterly "underground magazine" covering such topics as youth cultures, Paganism, Pantheism, poetry, and nature people. (This magazine is published only in Greek.) Sample copy: $4.00; one-year subscription: $22.00.

Asatru Today
Lewis Stead, editor
11160 Veirs Mill Road, L15-175
Wheaton, Maryland 20902

A quarterly journal of Germanic Paganism. Established in 1994 and digest size. One-year subscription: $15.00.

A.S.P.E.N. Leaves
Patti Nelson-Davis and Don Davis, editors
P.O. Box 16651
Phoenix, Arizona 85011

A newsletter for the Pagan community. Published eight times per year. Submissions and artwork are welcome. Write for more information.

Asynjur
P.O. Box 567
Granville, Ohio 43023

A journal of the northern goddesses. Sample copy: $3.00.

At the Crossroads
Jeanne Neath, editor
P.O. Box 112
St. Paul, Arkansas 72760

"Feminism, spirituality and new Paradigm Science exploring Earthly and unearthly reality." Sample copy: $6.50; one-year subscription (two biyearly issues): $24.00; Canadian and foreign subscriptions: $36.00.

Azrael Project Newsletter
Lorraine Chandler, publisher/editor
Westgate Press
5219 Magazine Street
New Orleans, Louisiana 70115
(504) 899-3077

"Dedicated to a macroscopic understanding of the Angel of Death." Published semi-annually. Sample copy: $5.00; one-year subscription: $10.00.

Baba Yaga News
  Pamela Getner, editor
  P.O. Box 330
  South Lee, Massachusetts 01260
  (413) 243-4036
  "A celebration of creative expression." Free sample copy; one-year subscription: $8.00; Canadian subscription: $10.00.

Being
  Marjorie Talarico, editor
  P.O. Box 417
  Oceanside, California 92054
  "A celebration of Spirit, Mind, and Body." Sample subjects: spirit-, God-, and Goddess-related, fantasy, sword, and sorcerer-(ess). Sample copy: $3.00.

Belladonna
  P.O. Box 935
  Simpsonville, South Carolina 29681
  Sample copy: $4.00.

Beltane Papers
  P.O. Box 29694
  Bellingham, Washington 98228
  "A Pagan/Feminist journal of women's spirituality." Articles, interviews, rituals, herbal lore, book reviews and more. *The Beltane Papers* exists to provide women with a safe place in which to explore the dimensions of our spiritual experience, and then to name it. Publishes quarterly. Submissions by women welcome; pays in copies. Sample copy: $8.50; one-year subscription: $21.00.

Beyond Bifrost
  Lori Johnson, editor
  P.O. Box 814
  Douglas, Michigan 49406
  (616) 857-4463

  A quarterly newsletter for individuals who are new to Odinism and Asatru. Free sample copy; one-year subscription: $5.00.

Black Moon Publishing
    P.O. Box 19469
    Cincinnati, Ohio 45219

The "largest open occult archive of manuscripts in the Western world." Send $1.00 for their current list.

Bridge Between the Worlds
    10 Royal Orchard Boulevard
    Box 53067
    Thornhill, Ontario L3T 7R9
    Canada

An international contact newsletter, published four times per year and "dedicated to older (pre-1970s) Witchcraft traditions." Sample copy: $3.00; one-year subscription: $10.00.

Calendar of Events
    c/o Larry Cornett, editor
    9355 Sibelius Drive
    Vienna, Virginia 22182

A newsletter of festivals, contacts, workshops, and retreats of interest to or sponsored by Neo-Pagans. One-year subscription: $4.50; Canadian subscription: $5.00.

Calendar of Moons
    Ben Sargent, editor
    Ninefold Press
    P.O. Box 2215
    Natick, Massachusetts 01760

A yearly "sacred lunar calendar in magazine format." It is available in Eastern, Central, and Pacific editions. Sample (one month): $1.00; one year: $9.00; Canadian subscription: $11.00.

The Cauldron
    Mike Howard, editor
    Caemorgan Cottage, Caemorgan Road
    Cardigan, Dyfed, SA43 1QU
    Wales

A "Pagan journal of the Old Religion, Wicca and Earth Mysteries." One-year subscription: $20.00 (cash only; checks and money orders are not accepted.)

Celtic Camper
P.O. Box 782
Tucson, Arizona 85702

"A quarterly journal of progressive Wiccan observation and opinion, and r/evolutionary eclectic Wiccan thought." One-year subscription: $7.00; two-year subscription: $13.00; foreign subscriptions: $10.00 (U.S. funds only).

C.E.M. News
P.O. Box 1652
Betnay, Oklahoma 73008

A "networking tool of the Children of the Earth Mother. A Neo Pagan newsletter of articles, art, poetry, and more. A forum for the Pagan Parent Network." Sample copy: $1.75; one-year subscription (eight issues): $12.00.

Changing Men
Michael Biernbaum, editor
P.O. Box 908
Madison, Wisconsin 53701
(608) 256-2565

A profeminist magazine serving the national men's movement. Established in 1979 and published three times per year. Sample copy: $7.00; subscription (four issues): $24.00.

Cincinnati Journal of Magick
c/o Black Moon Publishing
P.O. Box 19469
Cincinnati, Ohio 45219

Sample copy: $6.00.

Circle Network News
Dennis Carpenter, editor
P.O. Box 219
Mount Horeb, Wisconsin 53572
(608) 924-2216 (1 P.M. to 4 P.M. weekdays, Central Standard Time)

A quarterly newspaper of contemporary Paganism, Nature Spirituality, Wicca, Shamanism, and Goddess religion. They provide news, views, announcements, rituals, networking, and a "Magickal Marketplace." Free sample copy; one-year subscription: $15.00; Canadian and Mexican subscriptions: $20.00 (U.S. funds only).

Coming Out Pagan
Wordsmith Writing Services
P.O. Box 30811
Bethesda, Maryland 20824

A "quarterly newsletter for LesBiGay Pagans of all traditions. High-quality publication with an international readership. Networking, community resources, media reviews, fiction, poetry, Tarot, humor, and more. Artwork and short written submissions welcome. Confidentiality assured." Sample copy: $3.00; one-year subscription: $11.00; Canadian subscription: $13.00; other countries: $15.00 (U.S. funds only). Please make all checks and money orders payable to Wordsmith Writing Services.

Compost Newsletter
729 5th Avenue
San Francisco, California 94118

"A magazine of humor, satire, and bad taste, both in the Craft and out." Sample copy: $2.00 (please make all checks and money orders payable to V. Walker for CNL).

The Cosmic Calling
Raymond Mardyks, editor
P.O. Box 2841
Sedona, Arizona 86339

A galactic and Mayan astrology journal which offers its readers "a unique, expanded perspective regarding the relationship between the stars that make up our galaxy and the evolution of human consciousness as a part of the present planetary transformation." Sample copy: $5.00; one-year subscription: $18.00; all foreign subscriptions: $22.00.

Covenant of the Goddess Newsletter
P.O. Box 1226
Berkeley, California 94704

Established in 1975 and published eight times per year. Sample copy: $3.00; one-year subscription: $20.00.

Craft/Crafts
P.O. Box 441
Ponderay, Idaho 83852

"A quarterly publication of magickal projects for Wiccans and Pagans." Write for more information and subscription rates.

Crone Chronicles
Ann Kreilkamp, editor
P.O. Box 81
Kelly, Wyoming 83011
(307) 733-5409

A quarterly "journal of conscious aging" dedicated to reactivating the archetype of the Crone within modern Western culture. Named after the third aspect of the Triple Goddess, it "provides an open forum for exploring the range and depth of what the Crone evokes in us." Sample copy: $6.95; one-year subscription: $21.00.

Crystal Moon Metaphysical Digest
Firewalker and Talon, publishers/editors
P.O. Box 802
Matteson, Illinois 60443

An "international metaphysical Pagan digest, published by The Order of the Crystal Moon, an international Pagan fellowship." Sample copy: $6.50 (Canada and Mexico: $7.50); one-year subscription: $25.00 (Canada and Mexico: $30.00).

Curious Minds
Lady Hawke, editor
415 Campbell Avenue
West Haven, Connecticut 06516
(203) 932-1193

A quarterly newsletter "for Witches, by Witches." Sample copy: $2.00; one-year subscription: $8.00.

Dalriada Magazine
Sammy McSkimming, editor
Dun Na Beatha, 2 Brathwic Place
Brodick, Isle of Arran KA278BN
Scotland
(40) 0770-302532

A quarterly magazine focusing on the native Celtic traditions of Ireland and Scotland. Sample copy: $7.00; one-year subscription: $15.00.

Daughters of Inanna

Teri Viereck, editor
P.O. Box 81804
Fairbanks, Alaska 99708

Established in 1987, this Pagan newsletter is published eight times per year. Sample copy: $2.00; one-year subscription: $10.00. Canadian subscription: $12.00.

Daughters of Nyx

Kim Antieau, editor
P.O. Box 1100
Stevenson, Washington 98648

A quarterly "magazine of Goddess stories, mythmaking, and Fairy Tales" from a feminist, matristic, non-patriarchal point of view. Sample copy: $4.50; one-year subscription: $8.00; two-year subscription: $14.00; Canadian subscription: $24.00.

Dharma Combat

P.O. Box 20593
Sun Valley, Nevada 89433

"An unedited reader-written forum about religion, metaphysics, and spirituality." Sample copy: $2.00.

Diipetes (For the Defense of the Ancient Spirit)

D. Pastelakos, editor
P.O. Box 20037
Athens GR-11810
Greece

"The first openly Pagan journal to be published in Greece." (This magazine is published only in Greek.) Sample copy: $5.00; one-year subscription: $25.00 (United States and Canada); European subscriptions: $20.00; elsewhere: $22.00.

Dragon Chronicle

Moondancer and Star, editors
P.O. Box 3369
London, SW6 6JN
England

A Pagan journal of the Dragon Trust, published twice each year. Sample copy: £2.50; one-year subscription: £7.00.

Eagle's Spirit
917½ 6th Street
Clarkston, Washington 99403

A monthly New Age newsletter. One-year subscription: $10.00.

Earth Circle News
P.O. Box 1938
Sebastopol, California 95473
(707) 829-8586

"A beautiful twenty-page quarterly devoted to issues of interest to the circling community—Wiccan, Pagan, women's and men's circles and lodges, drumming and healing circles, new and full moon groups—in short, nonhierarchical, Earth-centered Spirit groups that gather with an intent to heal and celebrate this Earthly existence." A free back-issue sample copy is sent upon request. One-year subscription: $15.00.

Earth Spirit
Azuel Crow, editor
P.O. Box 365
Medford, Massachusetts 02155
(617) 395-1023; fax: (617) 396-5066

A newsletter of Pagan culture. Articles, interviews, book reviews, letters column, announcement of Earth Spirit events, and other items of interest. Sample copy: $2.00; one-year subscription: $15.00 (includes membership in Earth Spirit).

Earth Spirit Star
P.O. Box 1965
Colorado Springs, Colorado 80901

The official magazine of Earth Spirit Pagans (E.S.P.). Published quarterly. One-year subscription: $16.00 (U.S. funds only).

Egyptian Religion Newsletter
Neter
P.O. Box 290011
Tampa, Florida 33687

Eidolon
P.O. Box 4117
Ann Arbor, Michigan 48106

Eklektikos
Jackie Ramirez, editor
788 Harrison Street
Lebanon, Ohio 97355

An "eclectic reader participation journal," published six times per year. Sample copy: $3.00; one-year subscription: $15.00; foreign subscriptions: $25.00.

Eldar's Cauldron
P.O. Box 28692
Columbus, Ohio 43228

"An international publication of magick, musings, and miscellaneous." Published eight times per year on the Greater and Lesser Sabbats. Sample copy: $1.50; one-year subscription: $12.00.

Emania
Ford and Bailie
P.O. Box 138
Belmont, Massachusetts 02178

Emerging Self
Mary Paruszkiewicz, editor
129 C. Lucille Court
Bartlett, Illinois 60103

A quarterly newsletter "for anyone interested in alternative healing from all walks of life, including Pagan and Goddess spirituality." Send two first-class stamps for free sample copy; one-year subscription: $13.00.

Enchante
c/o John Yohalem, editor
30 Charlton Street, no. 6F
New York, New York 10014

"The journal for the Urbane Pagan." Sample copy: $3.50; one-year subscription: $12.00.

Enchanting News
   Frank Hedgecock, editor
   P.O. Box 145
   Marion, Connecticut 06444
   (203) 621-3579

   A quarterly Pagan magazine published in honor of the God and the Goddess. Sample copy: $2.50; one-year subscription: $14.00; Canadian subscription: $18.00.

Familiars
   Winter Wren, editor
   P.O. Box 247
   Normal, Illinois 61761
   (309) 888-4689

   A quarterly magazine for Eclectic Pagans of all ages, and a newsletter for the Illinois chapter of WARD. Write for more information and subscription rates.

Fertile Soil
   Elizabeth B.J. Lord, publisher/editor
   P.O. Box 503
   Swanton, Ohio 43558
   (419) 826-4414; Fax: (419) 826-1062

   A journal of writings that explore the spiritual nature of the universe. Each issue contains reader-written articles, channeled material from ascended masters, creative writing and poetry. Sample copy: $1.00; one-year subscription: $20.00.

Festive Circles Update
   c/o GLPC
   P.O. Box 26442
   Oklahoma City, Oklahoma 73126

   A newsletter published by the Gay and Lesbian Pagan Coalition. Sample copy: $3.00.

Fireheart
   Myrriah Lavin, editor
   P.O. Box 462
   Maynard, Massachusetts 01754
   (617) 395-1023; Fax: (617) 396-5066

"A journal of magick and spiritual transformation. *Fireheart* is published by the Earth Spirit Community, a national network of Pagans and other Earth-centered people." Sample copy: $5.00; subscription (two issues): $10.00.

Free Spirit Rising
P.O. Box 5358
Laurel, Maryland 20726
(301) 604-6049

A quarterly newsletter of the Free Spirit Alliance. Established in 1986. Sample copy: $2.00; one-year subscription: $10.00.

From the Heart
c/o Kathryn Hinds, editor
728 Derrydown Way
Decatur, Georgia 30030

A journal of Pagan parenting, published approximately six times per year. Send one fifty-two-cent stamp for a free sample copy; one-year subscription: $13.00; Canadian subscription: $15.00; back issues: $2.00 each.

Georgian Newsletter
1980 Verde
Bakersfield, California 93304
Sample copy: $1.00.

Gnosis
Richard Smoley, editor
P.O. Box 14217
San Francisco, California 94114

A "journal of the Western Inner Traditions." Published four times per year; approximately eighty-eight pages per issue. Send a self-addressed stamped envelope for free information. Sample copy: $6.00; one-year subscription: $20.00; Canadian subscription: $25.00 (international money order or check drawn on a U.S. bank only).

Golden Isis Magazine
Gerina Dunwich, editor
P.O. Box 525
Fort Covington, New York 12937

A quarterly New Age and Neo-Pagan journal of mystical and Goddess-inspired poetry, Pagan art, Wiccan news and announcements, reviews, networking service, ads, and more. Established in California in 1980. Positive magick for solitaries and covens of all traditions, and a literary forum in which individuals from around the world can come together to share poetic visions and their special love for the Goddess and other Pagan deities. Articles, poetry, ritual outlines, spells, Witchy recipes, and artwork submissions are more than welcome. Golden Isis Press also publishes chapbooks (such as love magick, money spells, hex-breaking, etc.) and offers natal charts, Tarot card readings, spell-casting services (such as Love magick, money spells, hex-breaking, etc.), and *Circle of Shadows*, by Gerina Dunwich. Advertisers should write for classified and display ad rates. Will consider exchanging ads with other publications. Free Pagan and Wiccan contacts. Please include a self-addressed stamped envelope when submitting material for publication or requesting free guidelines and information. Sample copy: $3.00; one-year subscription: $10.00; Canadian subscription: $15.00 (U.S. funds only)

The Green Egg
P.O. Box 1542
Ukiah, California 95482

The quarterly journal of the Church of All Worlds. "The 1970's foremost magazine of Neo-Paganism has returned to deliver an interdisciplinary treasure trove: Shamanism, Goddess lore, psychic development, Gaea and environmental activism, suppressed history, alternative sexuality, plus an uncensored Readers Forum." Sample copy: $6.00; one-year subscription: $24.00; Canadian, Mexican, and Latin American subscriptions: $36.00.

Green Man
Diana Darling, editor
P.O. Box 641
Point Arena, California 95468
(707) 882-2052

"A magazine for Pagan men. Exploring the mysteries of Gods and Goddesses, rituals and myth creation that celebrate men's connection with one another, with women, and with the natural world."

Sample copy: $4.00; one-year subscription: $13.00; Canadian subscription: $18.00.

H.A.M. (How About Magick?)
Nemeton
P.O. Box 488
Laytonville, California 95454

A journal for Pagan youth.

Hallows
William D. Calhoun, editor
P.O. Box 5807
Athens, Ohio 45701

A journal of the Ordo Arcanorum Gradalis—a Gnostic Christo-Pagan Order of the Grail Quest. Subscriptions are free but available only to students and members of the Order.

The Hawthorn Spinner
Endymion Vervaine, editor
P.O. Box 706
Monticello, New York 12701

A quarterly magazine of ancient and modern Paganism, particularly Wicca. To receive a sample copy, please send a self-addressed stamped envelope and a donation of any amount.

Hazel Grove Musings
Shirley Dawson-Myers, editor
1225 E. Sunset Drive, no. 304
Bellingham, Washington 98226

A "quarterly journal of Pagan musings." Sample copy: $2.00; one-year subscription: $8.00.

The Hazel Nut
Linda Kerr, editor
P.O. Box 186
Auburn, Alabama 36831
(334) 212-4683

A quarterly journal of "Celtic spirituality and sacred trees. This publication features the trees associated with the lunar calendar, folklore, herbcraft, historical research, poetry, artwork, and reviews. Sample copy:

$4.50 (Canada: $4.75); one-year subscription: $13.00 to $22.00 (sliding scale); Canadian subscription: $14.00 to $23.00 (sliding scale).

Heart Dance
  Oshara, editor
  473 Miller Avenue
  Mill Valley, California 94941
  (415) 383-2525

  A monthly events calendar for the San Francisco Bay Area's spiritual and New Age communities. Sample copy: $1.00; one-year subscription: $15.00 to $25.00 (sliding scale).

Heartsong Review
  Wahaba Heartsun, editor
  P.O. Box 5716
  Eugene, Oregon 97405

  Reviews of Pagan and spiritually-conscious music. Sample copy: $5.00; one-year subscription: $8.00; Canadian subscription: $10.00. (Subscribers receive a free hour-long sampler tape with each issue.)

Heavenly Fragrances
  c/o Midnight Angel, Inc.
  P.O. Box 951
  Old Bridge, New Jersey 08857

  A 5½″ × 8½″ magazine about magickal and astrological fragrances, serving to inform customers of some of the oils and incenses offered from Midnight Angel.

Hecate's Loom
  P.O. Box 5206, Station B
  Victoria, British Columbia V8R 6N4
  Canada
  (604) 477-8488

  "A Canadian Pagan quarterly celebrating the return of the Goddess. Includes articles, letters, prose and more." Write for more information and subscription rates.

Hermit's Lantern
  Rev. Paul V. Beyerl, editor
  P.O. Box 0691
  Kirkland, Washington 98083

A monthly educational newsletter published by the Hermit's Grove and containing information on basic metaphysical sciences: herbalism, Tarot, astrology, gems and minerals, ritualism, and others. Sample copy: $2.00; one-year subscription: $20.00.

The Higher Choice
Salanda, publisher/editor
P.O. Box 65
Neotsu, Oregon 97364

A monthly journal featuring astrology, a question and answer forum, fiction, evolutionary discussions, and more. Sample copy: free. One-year subscription: $12.00; two year subscription: $20.00.

Hole in the Stone: A Journal of the Wiccan Life
Rhiannon Asher and George Moyer, editors
2125 W. Evans
Denver, Colorado 80223

A national quarterly Pagan journal with a calendar of events serving the Colorado Pagan community. Contains poetry, art, reviews, rituals, and more. Sample copy: $2.00; one-year subscription: $12.00; Canadian subscription: $17.00.

Horns and Crescent
Meagan and Jennifer, coeditors
P.O. Box 622
Millis, Massachusetts 02054

"To create bridges within the Pagan community, not build walls." Calendar listings are free, subject to space limitations and editorial policies. One-year subscription (eight issues): $5.00.

Idunna
Thorfinn Einarsson, editor
c/o The Troth
P.O. Box 25637
Tempe, Arizona 85285

This quarterly magazine is "the official journal of the Ring of Troth." Covers heathen gods and goddesses, runes, sagas, and mythology. Sample copy: $7.00; one-year subscription: $24.00.

Intuitive Exploration
Gloria Reiser, publisher/editor
P.O. Box 561
Quincy, Illinois 62306

A bimonthly newsletter offering "a wide range of metaphysical and New Age thought." Editorial content includes articles, reviews of books and products, interviews, true life experiences of the mystical, and more. Sample copy: $3.00; one-year subscription (U.S., Canada and Mexico): $15.00; all other subscriptions: $25.00.

Is to Be!
P.O. Box 1055
Suisun City, California 94585

A quarterly newsletter for the sharing of ideas and information amongst practitioners of magick and those interested in magickal theory. For both the beginner and the advanced magician. Sample copy: $3.00; one-year subscription: $15.00; all foreign subscriptions: $25.00.

Ishpiming Magazine
Sage, editor
P.O. Box 340
Manitowish Waters, Wisconsin 54545
(715) 686-2372

An annual magazine for individuals who follow the path of Nature Spirituality. To receive a sample copy, send in a donation of any amount. One-year subscription: $12.00 donation is suggested.

Isian News
Lord Strathlock and Hon. Olivia Robertson, editors
Fellowship of Isis, Foundation Centre
Clonegal Castle, Clonegal Enniscorthy
Ireland

"Quarterly coverage of international Goddess-oriented Pagan news and contacts, available to members only. Apply for membership (no fees required)." Sample copy: $2.50 (£1.40); one-year subscription: $20.00 (£5.50).

Isis Connection
Isis, editor
P.O. Box 1636
Gresham, Oregon 97030

A monthly newsletter "to awaken, to expand consciousness, and raise awareness of the reality of the Oneness of all life." Editorial content includes channeled articles, essays, and reports of UFO sightings. Sample copy: $3.00; one-year subscription: $36.00 (sliding scale).

The Isis Papers
11666 Gateway Boulevard (no. 163)
Los Angeles, California 90064

A journal of poems, stories, art and meditations, published by the Iseum of the Isis Pelagia (Isis of the Sea). Sample copy: $8.00. Make checks payable to Laura Janesdaughter.

K.A.M.
P.O. Box 2513
Kensington, Maryland 20891

A journal of Traditional Wicca. Sample copy: $3.00.

Keltria: Journal of Druidism and Celtic Magick
Tony Taylor, editor
P.O. Box 48369
Minneapolis, Minnesota 55448

"This quarterly journal provides insight into Druidism and Celtic Magickal religions, and promotes Druidic education and fellowship through articles concerning the three Druidic paths of the Bard, the Seer, and the Druid. Theme articles, as well as reviews and letters. One-year subscription: $12.00.

Lady Letter
Michelle Vachosky, editor
P.O. Box 1107
Los Alamos, New Mexico 87544

The official newsletter of the Church of Our Lady of the Woods, published eight times per year. Free sample copy available upon request.

Leaves
Michael Ragan, editor
P.O. Box 765
Hanover, Indiana 47243

A newsletter containing information on the activities and research of the Temple of Danann. One-year subscription: $13.00.

Littlest Unicorn
c/o The Rowan Tree Church
9724 132nd Avenue N.E.
Kirkland, Washington 98033

A publication for children (newborn to ten years old) and Pagan parents. Published eight times per year on the Greater and Lesser Sabbats. Contains stories, artwork, poetry, and more. Sample copy: $1.50; one-year subscription: $9.75; sample packet: $5.00 (includes *The Littlest Unicorn*, *The Unicorn* [a publication for adults], and information on the Rowan Tree Church and its Mystery School).

Llewellyn New Worlds of Mind and Spirit
P.O. Box 64383
St. Paul, Minnesota 55164
(800) THE MOON

A magazine and catalog of astrology, magick, occult, Nature Spirituality and New Age books, tapes, and services. Reviews, articles, sales and events notices, calendar, answer column. Free sample copy upon request.

Llyr: The Magazine of Celtic Arts
3313 N. Mont Road
Baltimore, Maryland 21244

Magic Wand
P.O. Box 27164
Detroit, Michigan 48227

"A journal for serious, practicing Pagans. Magick, stone craft, herbalism, herstory, solitary craft, and much more!" Sample copy: $2.00; subscription (eight issues): $8.00.

Magical Blend
P.O. Box 11303
San Francisco, California 94101

The Magical Confluence
P.O. Box 230111
St. Louis, Missouri 63123
Sample copy: $3.00.

Magical Forest Gazette
Eileen Smith, editor
2072 N. University Drive
Pembroke Pines, Florida 33024
A quarterly newsletter of Wicca and Paganism. One-year subscription: $4.00.

Magickal Unicorn Messenger
817½ Park
Findlay, Ohio 45840
A Pagan and occult publication. Sample copy: $2.50; one-year subscription (four issues): $9.00.

Maiden Moon
2-919 10th Avenue North
Saskatoon, Saskatchewan S7K 3A3
Canada
A metaphysical quarterly published by a group of Neo-Pagan spiritualists. Provides a forum for communication and sharing between all individuals and groups that abide by the Wiccan Rede. One-year subscription: $12.00; Canadian subscription: $15.00.

Meyn Mamvro
Cheryl Straffon, editor
51 Carn Bosavern, St. Just
Penzance, Cornwall TR19 7QX
England
A twenty-four page magazine of Paganism and Earth mysteries. Sample copy: $5.00 (cash); one-year subscription: $15.00 (cash). Personal checks and money orders are not accepted.

Mezlim
Kenneth Deigh, editor
P.O. Box 19566
Cincinnati, Ohio 45219
(513) 791-0344

A quarterly magazine of "Wicca, Shamanism, Ceremonial Magick, Neo-Paganism and related New Aeonic practices." Sample copy: $6.00; one-year subscription: $20.00; Canadian subscription: $27.00.

The Midnight Drive
Silver Ravenwolf, editor
P.O. Box 1392
Mechanicsburg, Pennsylvania 17055

The monthly newsletter of the WPPA (Wiccan/Pagan Press Alliance). Sample copy: $4.00; one-year subscription: $15.00; Canadian subscription: $17.00.

Midwest Pagan Correspondence
Chris Thomas, editor
P.O. Box 160
Western Springs, Illinois 60558

The quarterly newsletter of the Midwest Pagan Council. Book reviews, recipes, articles, updates on council activities, and more. Free sample copy; one-year subscription: $3.00.

Mnemosyne's Scroll
Helena Aislin Anderson, editor
P.O. Box 1137
Bryn Mawr, Pennsylvania 19010

Published quarterly by the Coven of Oak and Willow. Sample copy: $1.50; one-year subscription: $5.00.

Moira
M. Jean Louis de Biasi, editor
B.P. 68, 33034 Bordeaux Cedex
France
Phone: 56-94-73-99

A quarterly magazine of occult traditions, including Witchcraft and Paganism. Published in French by the Circle of the Dragon. Sample copy: $6.00; one-year subscription: $20.00.

Moonweb
Amatheon, editor
P.O. Box 15461
Washington, D.C. 20003

"Synchronous rituals" for covens and solitaries worldwide. To receive a sample copy, send two first-class stamps.

Mystic Magick

Lara Light, editor
P.O. Box 387
Springfield, Oregon 97477

No standard subscription price. Send a self-addressed stamped envelope for free sample copy and more information.

Mystic Messenger

Iscara, editor
P.O. Box 294
Dallastown, Pennsylvania 17313
(717) 246-3634

Bimonthly newsletter containing articles, reviews, and listings of local events and national gatherings of interest to Wiccans and Pagans. Write for more information.

Newaeon Newsletter

G. M. Kelly, editor
P.O. Box 19210
Pittsburgh, Pennsylvania 15213

"A genuine Thelemic publication dedicated to the further establishment and defense of Thelema which, in part, exposes the lies of the greatest threat to Thelema: those who misrepresent themselves as Thelemites to further their petty personal goals at the expense of the truth." For more information, send $1.00 and a self-addressed stamped envelope (deductible from first order). Sample (current volume): $6.66; back issues: $7.77 each. (U.S. funds only; please make checks and money orders payable to G. M. Kelly.)

New Moon Rising

Scot Rhoads, editor
12345 S.E. Fuller Road, no. 119
Milwaukie, Oregon 97222

"A bimonthly magazine of magick and Wicca. Includes Pagan parenting, animal guides, Kabbala, Shamanism, Tarot, crystals, astrology, rituals, ceremonial magick, ancient and modern religion and more!"

Sample copy: $3.00; one-year subscription (six issues): $14.00; Canadian and Mexican subscriptions: $21.00; other countries: $30.00.

Night-by-Night
Gerard Spring, editor
P.O. Box 318
Milton, Massachusetts 02186
(617) 698-8330

A daily astrological guide, published once a month. Sample copy: $2.00; one-year subscription: $15.00; Canadian subscription: $18.00.

Night Scapes
Jay Barrymore and Gil Davis, editors
P.O. Box 4559
Mesa, Arizona 85211
(602) 898-3551

A bimonthly magazine of magick, Paganism, and the occult. Sample copy: $3.00; one-year subscription: $13.00; Canadian subscription: $15.00.

North Star
P.O. Box 878–887
Wasilla, Alaska 99687

"A newsletter for families who choose to teach their own, while following a Wiccan/Pagan spiritual path. Features include children's forum, news watch, reviews, poetry, recipes, networking." Sample copy: $1.00; one-year subscription (six issues): $12.00; Canadian and Mexican subscriptions: $18.00.

Northwind Network
P.O. Box 14902
Columbus, Ohio 43214

"A Pagan paper focusing on Goddess information, rituals, and networking. Reader participation encouraged." Sample copy: $1.50.

Of a Like Mind
Lynn Levy, editor
P.O. Box 6677
Madison, Wisconsin 53716
(608) 244-0072

"A women's spiritual newspaper and network dedicated to bringing together women following positive paths to spiritual growth. Its focus is on women's spirituality, Goddess religions, Paganism, and our Earth connections from a feminist perspective." Sample copy: $4.00; one-year subscription: $15.00 to $35.00 (sliding scale). Send a self-addressed stamped envelope for a free brochure.

Omega New Age Directory
     Rev. Dr. John Rodgers, editor
     6418 S. 39th Avenue
     Phoenix, Arizona 85041
     (602) 237-3213

A monthly New Age newspaper containing a calendar of events and a regional directory of groups and churches. Sample copy: $1.50; one-year subscription: $15.00.

Open Circle
     P.O. Box 060192
     Palm Bay, Florida 32906
     (407) 253-1473

A Wiccan newsletter based in central Florida. Information on events, networking, spirituality, Sabbat, herb lore, and more. To receive a free sample copy, send a self-addressed stamped envelope and two 32-cent stamps. One-year subscription: $10.00.

Open Ways
     P.O. Box 14415
     Portland, Oregon 97214
     (503) 239-8877

A newsletter for the Pagan communities in Oregon and the Pacific Northwest. Sample copy: $1.00; one-year subscription: $8.00.

Our Pagan Times
     Clover Welsh, editor
     P.O. Box 1471, Madison Square Station
     New York, New York 10159
     (212) 662-1080

A monthly newsletter for the Pagan community. Sample copy: $2.00; one-year subscription: $15.00.

Out of the Broom Closet
P.O. Box 2298
Athens, Ohio 45701
(614) 592-1755

A quarterly magazine of alternative spirituality, published by Pentamerous Publishing, a nonprofit organization. Sample copy: $4.00; one-year subscription: $13.00; Canadian subscription: $15.00.

Outer Court Communications
Sabrina, editor
P.O. Box 1366
Nashua, New Hampshire 03061
(603) 880-7237

A ten-page newsletter, established in 1980 and published once a year. Contains book reviews, rituals, information about Our Lady of Enchantment, and other material. One-year subscription: $12.00; Canadian subscription: $15.00.

Pacific Circle Newsletter
P.O. Box 9513
North Hollywood, California 91609

Free sample copy available upon request.

Pagan Dawn
Address: Pagan Federation
BM Box 7097
London WC1N 3XX
England

"A forty-page, illustrated quarterly magazine," established in 1971 and focusing on "British Wicca, Paganism, and Druidism." Each issue contains research articles, news, poetry, contacts, and information about groups, gatherings, and rituals throughout Great Britain and Europe. Sample copy: $7 00; one-year subscription: $25.00 (cash preferred, U.S. or Canadian currency).

Pagan Digest
D. J. Pruitt, editor
P.O. Box 18211
Encino, California 91316
(213) 653-1699

A quarterly, fifty-page Craft and Pagan magazine featuring a wide variety of articles, poetry, reviews, and feature topics. Readers are invited to share their input. This is a publication of the Educational Society for Pagans (formerly the Pallas Society). Sample copy: $3.00; one-year subscription: $14.00.

Pagan Free-Press Newsletter
Address: P.F.P.
Victor Brotte, editor
P.O. Box 55223
Tulsa, Oklahoma 74155

Pagan Nuus
P.O. Box 640
Cambridge, Massachusetts 02140

The newsletter of the Covenant of Unitarian Universalist Pagans. Articles, book and movie reviews, graphics, poetry, and more. Sample copy: $1.00 to $2.00 (sliding scale).

Pagan Pride
Gerina Dunwich, editor
Address: P.P.S.
c/o North Country Wicca
P.O. Box 264
Bombay, New York 12914

Established in 1996, this is the official biannual journal of the Pagan Poets Society (P.P.S.). It contains poetry, artwork, announcements, a Pagan networking service and more. Sample copy: $5.00 (U.S. funds only. Please make checks and money orders payable to Gerina Dunwich.) One-year subscription: free with membership in the Pagan Poets Society. To receive a membership application, send a self-addressed stamped envelope. (For additional information, see the Pagan Poets Society listing in the organizations section of this book.)

Pagans for Peace
Samuel E. Wagar, editor
P.O. Box 2205
Clearbrook, British Columbia V2T 3X8
Canada

A bimonthly newsletter of "Pagan theology, political networking, and resource reviews." Free sample copy; one-year subscription: $10.00.

Pagans in Recovery Quarterly
Bekki Shining BearHeart, editor
22 Palmer Street
Athens, Ohio 45701
(614) 592-6193

A quarterly, eclectic Pagan publication for Pagans recovering from addiction, abuse, or a dysfunctional upbringing. Sample copy: $2.50; one-year subscription: $8.50.

P.A.N. Pipes
Lyle A. Austin, editor
P.O. Box 17933
Phoenix, Arizona 85011

"The official publication of the Pagan Arizona Network." Contains articles, spells, book reviews, and more. Published six times per year. Sample copy: $3.00; one-year subscription: $15.00.

Panegyria
Pete Pathfinder, editor
P.O. Box 409
Index, Washington 98256
(206) 793-1945

"A journal of the Aquarian Tabernacle Church. Published eight times per year on the major holidays. News of interest to Pagans in the Pacific Northwest and beyond." Send three 32-cent stamps to receive a free sample copy. Back issues: $2.00 each.

Pantheos
Joe Lawrence Lembo, editor
P.O. Box 9543
Santa Fe, New Mexico 87504

A nationwide personal networking newsletter for gay and bisexual Pagan men. Published quarterly. One-year subscription: $15.00; Canadian subscription: $16.00.

Psychic Pathways
P.O. Box 418
Woodmere, New York 11598
A "*Now* Age newsletter." One-year subscription: $15.00.

Psychic Reader
2210 Harold Way
Berkeley, California 94704
(510) 644-1600

Quest
Marian Green, editor
BCM–SCL Quest
London WC1N 3XX
England
Established in 1970. A quarterly newsletter of modern natural and ritual magick, book reviews, events, divination, training, and more. Sample copy: $4.00; one-year subscription: $20.00/£8 (cash).

Rainbow City Express
P.O. Box 8447
Berkeley, California 94707
"An eclectic, interfaith quarterly of true spiritual experiences, Great Mother encounters, Kundalini, higher consciousness and more." Sample copy: $6.00; one-year subscription: $24.00.

Raising the Sacred Serpent
Address: Hanah Leia
5051 E. Highway 98, no. 212
Destin, Florida 34698
A "journal and guidebook from the Temple of Hanah Leia. Documents inspirational relationship between a priestess and her beloved snake. Includes firsthand information on the care and feeding of sacred serpents." To receive a copy, send $7.50 plus $1.50 for shipping. (Please make checks and money orders payable to Hanah Leia.)

Razing the Stakes
Constance DeBinero and Elsa Drecowin, editors
P.O. Box 1646
Santa Cruz, California 95061

The quarterly magazine of The Index (a Pagan network servicing Santa Cruz and the central California coast). Contains articles, columns, reviews, poetry, invocations, and recipes. Sample copy: $3.00; one-year subscription: $15.00 (please make checks and money orders payable to The Index.)

Reclaiming
P.O. Box 14404
San Francisco, California 94114

A quarterly newsletter "dedicated to unifying spirit and politics." Sample copy: $2.00; one-year subscription: $6.00 to $25.00 (sliding scale).

Red Garters International
Allyn Wolfe, editor
P.O. Box 162046
Sacramento, California 95816

"The official voice of the New Wiccan Church, published at least eight times per year." Sample copy: $1.00; one-year subscription (United States and Canada): $10.00; foreign subscription: $12.00 surface, $20.00 airmail. (Please make checks and money orders payable to N.W.C.)

The Red Queen
603 W. 13th Street, no. 1A-132
Austin, Texas 78701

"A quarterly journal of Goddess religion, magick, Feminism, creativity, and more for women who never make bargains." Sample copy: $3.50; one-year subscription: $13.00.

Rosegate Journal
P.O. Box 5967
Providence, Rhode Island 02903

The Runestone
Stephen McNallen and Maddy Hutter, editors
P.O. Box 445
Nevada City, California 95959

A quarterly journal of the ancient northern European religion known as Asatru. Sample copy: $2.50; one-year subscription: $10.00.

Sacred Circle
Vilija Witte
Romuva/Canada
P.O. Box 232, Station D
Etobicoke, Ontario M9A 4X2
Canada

A journal focusing on Baltic Paganism.

Sacred Grove News
Janette Copeland and Kalman Mannis, editors
16845 N. 29th Avenue, no. 1346
Phoenix, Arizona 85023

"The official newsletter of the Divine Circle of the Sacred Grove Church and School of the Old Religion." Free sample copy upon request. One-year subscription: $2.00.

Sacred Heart Magazine
Bried Foxsong, editor
c/o Wyrdd Enterprises
P.O. Box 72
Kenmore, New York 14217

Sacred Record
Route no. 1, Box 7
Willcox, Arizona 85643

A publication of the Peyote Way Church of God. Write for information regarding sample copy and subscription rates.

Sacred Serpent
P.O. Box 232, Station D
Etobicoke, Ontario M9A 4X2
Canada

A quarterly publication focusing on the Baltic and Slavic traditions. One-year subscription: $10.00; overseas: $15.00. Please make checks and money orders payable to Iron Wolf.

Sage Woman
Anne Newkirk Niven, editor
P.O. Box 641
Point Arena, California 95468
(707) 882-2052; fax: (707) 882-2793

Established in 1986. An eighty-page quarterly magazine of women's spirituality, celebrating the Goddess in every woman. Free sample copy sent upon request. One-year subscription: $18.00; two-year subscription: $33.00 (California residents add 7¼ percent sales tax).

Sanctuary Circles
P.O. Box 219
Mount Horeb, Wisconsin 53572

The newsletter of the Circle Sanctuary Community. It is edited by the staff of Circle and published eight times per year. Free sample copy upon request. One-year subscription: $10.00 minimum donation (free to those who are active members).

The Seeker
John Morris, editor
P.O. Box 3326
Ann Arbor, Michigan 48106
(313) 665-3522

A monthly newsletter focusing on Earth-centered religion based in southeast Michigan. Sample copy: $1.00; one-year subscription: $10.00; Canadian subscription: $15.00.

The Serpent's Tail
Karin Lorenz Clark, editor
P.O. Box 07437
Milwaukee, Wisconsin 53207
(414) 769-1785

A quarterly newsletter focusing on Earth and Goddess-oriented religion. Sample copy: $1.00; one-year subscription: $10.00; foreign subscription: $15.00.

Shamanka
Vee Van Dam, editor
53 Hallett Way
Bude, Cornwall EX23 8PG
England
Phone: (0288) 356457

A newsletter of Shamanism, androgyny, letters, Kaiana channelings, reviews, ads, and more. Sample copy: $1.00 (50 p.); one-year subscription: $4.00 (£2.75).

Shared Transformation
El Collie, editor
P.O. Box 5562
Oakland, California 94605

A newsletter for persons experiencing spiritual emergence and kundalini awakening. Editorial content includes such topics as astrology, cross-cultural traditions, dreams, folklore, healing and health, kundalini, meditation, mysticism, mythology, parapsychology, psychic phenomena, Shamanism and spirituality. Send a self-addressed stamped envelope to receive a free sample copy. One-year subscription: $12.00.

Silver Chalice Magazine
Steven R. Smith, editor
P.O. Box 196
Thorofare, New Jersey 08086

A quarterly newsletter of Paganism and Wicca. Sample copy: $2.00; one-year subscription: $6.00; Canadian subscription: $7.00.

Silver Pentagram, The
Reed Dunwich, editor
P.O. Box 9776
Pittsburgh, Pennsylvania 15229

"A Witchcraft journal serving the Craft through its members." It contains ads, articles, poetry, and is a member of the Wiccan/ Pagan Press Alliance. Sample copy: $1.50; one-year subscription: $6.00 (outside of the United States, add $3.00).

Societé
Courtney Willis, editor
c/o Technicians of the Sacred
1317 N. San Fernando Boulevard, Suite 310
Burbank, California 91504

A magazine of "Voudou and other Neo-African religious systems, magick, art, and culture." One-year subscription (three issues): $15.00.

Solitary, By Choice or by Chance
De-Anna Alba, editor
P.O. Box 6091
Madison, Wisconsin 53716
(608) 244-0072

A quarterly journal published for solitary Wiccans and Pagans. Sample copy: $3.50; one-year subscription: $15.00 to $36.00 (sliding scale).

Solitary Path
Kazan Clark, editor
Route 1, Box 47-A
Havana, Arkansas 72842
(501) 476-2071

An eclectic bimonthly newsletter (formerly *Wiccan Times*) for the solitary practitioner. Sample copy: $1.00; one-year subscription: $13.00; Canadian subscription: $18.00.

Somnial Times
Mike Banys, editor
P.O. Box 561
Quincy, Illinois 63206
(217) 222-9082

A bimonthly publication focusing on dreams and related states. One-year subscription: $10.00; all foreign subscriptions: $12.00.

Songs of the Dayshift Foreman
Gwyneth Cathyl-Bickford, editor
Box 1607
Aldergrove, British Columbia V4W 2V1
Canada

A journal of modern Witchcraft. Wiccans are invited to submit material. Sample copy: $2.00 (cash only); one-year subscription: $15.00 to $20.00 (sliding scale). Please make checks and money orders payable to Susan Davidson.

Soulmate News
Jim Thompson, Jr., editor
P.O. Box 769
Sandia Park, New Mexico 87047

A networking newsletter for single women and men seeking their spiritual life partner. Contains extensive male and female profile lists, articles, poetry, and reviews of books and tapes. For more information, send a self-addressed stamped envelope.

Spinning in the Light
850 S. Rancho Drive, no. 2-355
Las Vegas, Nevada 89106
"A magazine for the New Age of spiritual enlightenment." Published eight times per year by the Guardians of Light and Life/Clan of the Spider. Articles, predictions, horoscopes, recipes, poetry, and more. One-year subscription: $18.00.

Spirit of the Moment
Lance Lewey, editor
P.O. Box 26778
St. Louis Park, Minnesota 55426
(612) 936-9562
A newsletter serving the Twin Cities Pagan community. Sample copy: $2.00; one-year subscription: $16.00.

Symphony
Aline H. Simon, editor
P.O. Box 27465
San Antonio, Texas 78227
A quarterly Pagan-oriented magazine of magick and harmony. Sample copy: $3.50; one-year subscription: $12.00.

Talking Leaves
1430 Willamette, no. 367
Eugene, Oregon 97401

Talking Stick
Adrian Schoenherr, editor
P.O. Box 4274
Ann Arbor, Michigan 48106
A bimonthly newsletter serving the Pagan community of Ann Arbor. Sample copy: $2.00; one-year subscription: $10.00.

Talking Stick
Pandora and Babylon, editors
P.O. Box 3719
London SW17 8X7
England
(081) 707-3473

A quarterly magazine focusing on Paganism, occultism, magick, and mythology. Sample copy: $5.25 (£2.80); one-year subscription: $20.00 (£10.00).

Tamulet, The
c/o Carole J. Preisach, editor
5545 Mission Road
Fallon, Nevada 89406
(702) 423-5049

A quarterly eight-page newsletter published in connection with the Parapsychology Special Interest Group of American Mensa, Ltd. Sample copy: $1.50; one-year subscription: $7.00; Canadian subscription: $7.50.

Tarot Network News
Box 104
Sausalito, California 94966

Tarot News
Gloria Reiser and Lola Lucas, editors
P.O. Box 561
Quincy, Illinois
(217) 222-9082

A bimonthly newsletter for both the beginner and the advanced Tarot enthusiast. Sample copy: $3.00; one-year subscription (U.S., Canada and Mexico): $15.00; all other subscriptions: $25.00.

TGG: International Journal of Crystal Enlightenment
c/o The Unicorn Coven
P.O. Box 219
Galveston, Indiana 46932

A quarterly of spells, runes, Shamanism, contacts, and more. Sample copy: $5.00.

Thesmophoria
P.O. Box 11363
Oakland, California 94611

The "voice of the new women's religion. Goddess lore, spells, sacred poetry, art, networking." To receive a free sample copy, send a self addressed stamped envelope along with your request.

Think

P.O. Box 286

Prides Crossing, Massachusetts 01965

"A new Pagan magazine, printing articles intended to provoke your thought processes." Published quarterly. Single issue: $3.75; photocopied sample: $1.00.

Thunderbow II

P.O. Box 185

Wheatridge, Colorado 80034

A monthly publication of Earth-religion and spirit-sciences from the Church of Seven Arrows. One-year subscription: $15.00.

T.I.P.

c/o EarthSpirit

Buffie Cafarella, editor

P.O. Box 365

Medford, Massachusetts 02155

(617) 395-1023

A networking newsletter for Pagan teenagers. (T.I.P. stands for Teens Into Paganism) Sample copy: $1.00; one-year subscription: $5.00.

Touchstone Newsletter

Address to: Lady Moonshadow

P.O. Box 975

Minot, North Dakota 58702

A monthly newsletter covering "all positive New Age topics." Reader participation, barter, penpals, poetry, recipes, and spells. Sample copy: $1.00 and a long self-addressed stamped envelope.

Trends and Predictions

Patrick O'Connell, publisher/editor

5610 Essex Drive N.W.

Albuquerque, New Mexico 87114

A semi-annual newsletter that focuses on current trends and predictions relating to the paranormal and metaphysical. Sample copy: $1.00; one-year subscription: $4.00.

True North
c/o The Denali Institute
P.O. Box 671510
Chugiak, Alaska 99567

A monthly journal that provides the reader with "practical techniques in the application of Northern spiritual traditions for freedom of mind and spirit." Six-month subscription: $11.00; one-year subscription: $19.00

Tsujigiri
Greg Carden, editor
501 Kirkwood Drive
Northport, Alabama 35476

A newsletter, "Orthodox Discordian Zine," of religion and humor. Free sample copy or subscription.

U.F.O. Newsclipping Service
Lucius Farish, publisher/editor
2 Caney Valley Drive
Plumerville, Arkansas 72127

A monthly publication reprinting current press reports on unidentified flying objects and other unexplained phenomena (such as Bigfoot, the Loch Ness Monster, cattle mutilations and so forth.) Sample copy: $5.00; one-year subscription: $55.00; Canadian subscription: $70.00; all other subscriptions: $80.00.

Unarius Light Journal
Dr. Charles Spiegel, executive editor
145 S. Magnolia Avenue
El Cajon, California 92020
(619) 444-7062; fax: (619) 444-9637

A quarterly publication of the Unarius Academy of Science (established in 1954). It features articles about individual psychic experiences, reincarnation and consciousness. Sample copy: $7.00; one year subscription: $30.00.

Unicorn

Rev. Paul V. Beyerl, editor
P.O. Box 0691
Kirkland, Washington 98083

Established in 1976. A Wiccan newsletter, published eight times per year by the Rowan Tree Church. Member of the Wiccan/Pagan Press Alliance (WPPA). Contains letters, articles, poetry, ritual outlines, book reviews, and a few ads. One-year subscription: $10.00.

Unknown Newsletter

c/o Luna Ventures
P.O. Box 398
Suisun, California 94585

A newsletter about "various unexplained phenomena, UFOs, and Witchcraft." Sample copy: $2.00.

Up Close

P.O. Box 12280
Mill Creek, Washington 98082
fax: (206) 485-7926

Articles and reviews of New Age and alternative publications. Published four times per year by Darla Sims Publications. Sample copy: $10.00; one-year subscription: $40.00; Canadian subscription: $45.00; all other subscriptions: $50.00.

Voice of the Anvil

P.O. Box 060672
Palm Bay, Florida 32906
(407) 722-0291

A monthly newsletter of Pagan and Wiccan networking in Florida for groups, gatherings, workshops, and seminars. Free sample copy available upon request. One-year subscription: $6.00.

The Web

Amber Vargringar, editor
P.O. Box 924
Springfield, Missouri 65801
(417) 865-5903

A monthly Wiccan and Pagan newsletter designed for networking. One-year subscription: $13.00.

Wheel of Hekate
P.O. Box 247
Normal, Illinois 61761

"A Pagan journal dedicated to excellence!" Fifty pages or more, published quarterly. Sample copy: $6.50; one-year subscription: $22.00; back issues: $7.50 each. Write for airmail and foreign rates.

Wicca-Brief
Arkana, editor
Georgstrasse 4
22041 Hamburg
Germany
Phone: (040) 687623

A Wiccan newsletter published in German eight times per year. Established in 1988. Sample copy: $5.00; one-year subscription: $40.00.

The Wiccan
BM Box 7097
London WC1N 3XX
England

The quarterly journal of the Pagan Federation. Sample copy: $6.00 (cash only); one-year subscription: $18.00 (£10.00).

Wiccan Rede
Merlin and Morgana, editors
P.O. Box 473
3700 Al Zeist, Holland

An "English/Dutch Craft magazine featuring in-depth articles on Craft Heritage, symbolism, archetypal images, natural magick, elemental forces, and seasonal tides; discussions about the Craft today; news, book reviews, and ads." Published quarterly. One-year subscription: $15.00 (airmail) or £8.00 (EEC countries). Cash only. Personal checks are not accepted.

Wild and Weedy (A Journal of Herbology)
Doreen Shababy, editor
P.O. Box 508
Clark Fork, Idaho 83011
(208) 266-1492

A twenty-eight page, quarterly journal of herbology for Pagans and Wiccans interested in creative herbcraft, wholistic healing, organic gardening, and other topics. Contains poetry, book reviews, contacts, and resources. Sample copy: $3.00; one-year subscription: $13.00; Canadian subscription: $15.00.

Wild Magick Bulletin
P.O. Box 1082
Bloomington, Indiana 47402

The official publication of the Elf Lore Family (E.L.F.). Contains articles on ecology, Earth religion, Tao, and more. One-year subscription (four issues): $8.00.

Winged Chariot
c/o Tracey Hoover
P.O. Box 1718
Milwaukee, Wisconsin 53201

A newsletter devoted to the Tarot. Sample copy: $2.00; one-year subscription: $10.00.

Wisdom in the Wind
P.O. Box 92
Burley, Idaho 83318
(208) 678-4526

A magazine for "seekers and newcomers of the Beauty Way of Pagan enlightenment." Write for more information and sample copy and subscription rates.

Witches' Almanac
P.O. Box 348
Cambridge, Massachusetts 02238

An annual almanac of occult lore and legend, astrology, rituals, spells, and recipes, including a "Moon Calendar" of Wiccan festivals and lunar phases; $7.45 for each issue (includes postage). Canadian orders: $8.45.

Witch's Page
160 Carriage Lane
Chicago Heights, Illinois 60411
Sample copy: $1.00.

Wodenwood
P.O. Box 33284
Minneapolis, Minnesota 55433

"A quarterly Neo-Pagan newsletter. Articles, rituals, book reviews, and more." Write for more information and sample copy and subscription rates.

Wood and Water
Daniel Cohen and Jan Henning, editors
77 Parliament Hill
London NW3 2TH
England

A "Goddess-centered, feminist influenced Pagan quarterly newsletter. Sample copy: $3.00 (£1.25); one-year subscription: $10.00 (£6.00). (Cannot accept checks or money orders not in pound sterling.)

Woman of Power
P.O. Box 2785
Orleans, Massachusetts 02653

A "quarterly magazine of feminism, spirituality, and politics. Features feminist visionaries and activists in articles, interviews, artwork, photography." Sample copy: $9.00; one-year subscription: $30.00. Write for information regarding Canadian and overseas rates.

Wyrd
Goldie Brown, editor
P.O. Box 624
Monroeville, Pennsylvania 15146

A quarterly newsletter of poetry relating to the occult, mysticism, and Nature Spirituality. Submissions should be no longer than forty-five lines (or one page) of previously unpublished material, preferably with a cover letter containing a brief biography. Poets whose work is published in *Wyrd* will receive a complimentary copy of that issue and may request additional copies at the special writers' discount of $3.00 each. Sample copy: $5.00; one-year subscription: $20.00.

Wyrrd Word
c/o Sandra McNally, editor
P.O. Box 510521
Melbourne Beach, Florida 32951

Published five times per year as "a bridge between Wiccans, eclectic Pagans, and the New Age community." Sample copy: $3.00; one-year subscription: $15.00; Canadian subscription: $18.00.

Yap'n (Yet Another Pagan Newsletter)
Duncan, editor
P.O. Box 02089
Columbus, Ohio 43202
(614) 265-8862

A bimonthly magazine for the Pagan community. Calendar of events, poetry, astrology, editorials, and more. Sample copy: $2.00; one-year subscription: free with $15.00 membership in the Pagan Community Council of Ohio.

Yggdrasil
Prudence Priest, editor
537 Jones Street, no. 165
San Francisco, California 94102

"A quarterly journal focusing on Heathen culture, ethos, religion, mythology, and runes." Sample copy: $2.00; one-year subscription: $6.00 (United States and Canada); foreign subscriptions: $8.00. (Please make checks and money orders payable to Freya's Folk.)

6

ASTROLOGY

"The contemplation of celestial things will make a man both
speak and think more sublimely and magnificently when he
descends to human affairs."

—CICERO

Astrology, also known as "the science of the stars," dates back to
the most ancient of times, but its popularity continues to remain
strong in the present day (and I'm confident that it will continue on
into the twenty-first century and probably beyond).

Many individuals, myself included, believe that the heavenly bodies
exert a mystical influence over the personalities, daily activities, and
even the destinies of all humans. If astrology didn't work, I'm sure
public interest in it would have died out centuries ago.

Astrology is perhaps the most mainstream of all the occult sciences,
to which the horoscope columns that appear in nearly every major
newspaper across the country give evidence. In most bookstores as-

trology books abound, and even famous celebrities and presidents have been known to consult professional astrologers for guidance and advice pertaining to their careers and love lives. Throughout the world numerous astrological societies, dating services, and chart-preparing businesses have been established, and every effort has been made to include the listings of each and every one in this section. (If it's in the stars, chances are it's in here as well!)

Arizona

American Federation of Astrologers, Inc.
P.O. Box 22040
Tempe, Arizona 85282

Astro-Logic
Box 37053
Phoenix, Arizona 85069
(602) 841-4916

California

Cosmic Connections
P.O. Box 22
Corona Del Mar, California 92660

Write for information on their "Star Talk" astrology tapes. They accept Visa and MasterCard.

Halloran Software
P.O. Box 75713
Los Angeles, California 90075

Astrology software for IBM, PC, and both DOS and Windows. For both the professional and the hobbyist. For a free catalog, write to the above address or call: (800) SEA-GOAT. (California residents call: (818) 501-6515.)

Simply Astrological
P.O. Box 6894
Pico Rivera, California 90661

Colorado

The Luna Connection
P.O. Box 21164
Boulder, Colorado 80308

"Reclaiming Archaic Heritage through Astrology." Woman-centered reports: natal, lunar, transit, or relationship (friends or lovers). Forecast horoscope. Catalog of custom reports and the meaning of the Luna Connection: $5.00 (credited to your first order).

Connecticut

A.C.S.
P.O. Box 958
Branford, Connecticut 06405

For a free brochure on astrology reports for yourself or your loved ones, write to the above address or call: (800) 839-9227.

Florida

Cosmic Corner/The Psychic Network
Box 499
Deerfield Beach, Florida 33443
Catalog: $2.00.

Illinois

Devon Astrology and Crystals Shop
11 E. Washington Street
Chicago, Illinois 60602
(312) 855-1853

Star Sage
P.O. Box 342
East Machias, Maine 04630
(800) STARSAGE

A complete astrological service offering in-depth personal life readings, compatibility reports, progressed reports addressing a specific concern or area of life, and more. Using the latest in astrological technology, they construct natal charts and carefully delineate the data to unfold the intricate pattern of a person's life as reflected by the heavens. Call or write for a free brochure and order form.

Massachusetts

A.C.A. Inc.
Box 395
Weston, Massachusetts 02193

For price information regarding natal charts, please write to the above address.

Astrolabe
Box 1750
Brewster, Massachusetts 02631
(800) 843-6682

Call or write for information about their top-quality astrology software for IBM, Windows, MS-DOS, and the Macintosh.

Michigan

Visions
P.O. Box 7043
Marquette, Michigan 49855

Missouri

Computer Astrology, Numerology, and Handwriting Compatibility Studies
2241 S. Grand Boulevard
St. Louis, Missouri 63103
(314) 776-1130

The Psychic Shop
5311 State Avenue
Kansas City, Missouri 64112
(816) 287-9719

New York

Golden Isis
P.O. Box 525
Fort Covington, New York 12937

All horoscopes hand-prepared by a professional Wiccan astrologer. Send birthdate, place, and exact time (if known) along with a check or money order for any of the following services: complete natal chart (includes planetary position chart, detailed personality profile, information on your positive and negative traits, love life, and career): $50.00; astrological compatibility reading (send birth data of both persons): $65.00; chart showing the position of the planets at the moment of your birth: $5.00. To find out your rising sign (ascendant) or the position of any planet at the time of your birth, send complete birth data, $1.00, and a self-addressed stamped envelope.

New York Astrology Center
350 Lexington Avenue
New York, New York 12452
(212) 949-7211

Ohio

Celestial Gateway
15400 Pearl Road
Strongsville, Ohio 44136
(216) 238-5731

Northern Ohio Valley Astrologers
c/o John Milam
P.O. Box 1
Lafferty, Ohio 43951
(614) 968-3366

Vermont

Abbe Bassett
P.O. Box 17
Essex Junction, Vermont 05453
Personal astrology services.

Washington

Rev. Paul V. Beyerl
The Hermit's Grove
9724 132nd Avenue N.E.
Kirkland, Washington 98033
Professional astrologer since 1976 offers natal chart interpretations, transit and progressed charts, relationship interpretations, and astrology courses. Write for fee scale (sliding fee and barter may be available).

United Kingdom

Astrological Association of Great Britain
BM Astrology
London WC1N 3XX
England

Faculty of Astrological Studies
Hook Cottage
Vines Cross, Heathfield
Sussex TN21 9EN
England

Telephone and Computer Resources

Matrix Software
(800) PLANETS
Call for a free catalog of astrology programs designed for home computers.

Stargazers
An astrological dating service for individuals desiring to "meet others on a spiritual path." To receive a free sample personals newsletter, call: (800) 782-7497.

7

HERBS

Herbs are magickal indeed. From their use in the flying ointments and love philtres of olden times to their use in the healing remedies of modern Witches and Shamans, herbs have always had a strong tie to Paganism and the Craft of the Wise.

Herbs seem to "vibrate" with mystical properties, and what Witch's kitchen would be complete without its herbs for potions, spellcraft, and rituals? Imagine a good old-fashioned cauldron brew without any herbs. You'd have to settle for something less appealing, such as eye of newt and wing of bat! Of course I'm joking, but seriously, herbs are an important part of the Craft and many of the more esoteric ones (mandrake, for example) can be quite difficult, if not downright impossible, to find at the local herb farm, health food store, gardening center, or in your supermarket's herbs and spices section. This is why I have included this section, devoted entirely to herbs and where to obtain them.

For additional dealers who specialize in herbs (both the ordinary and Witchy types) see Section 8, "Magickal and Metaphysical Shops," and also Section 9, "Mail Order." There you will find many companies that carry a wide variety of herbs, as well as other items, and probably have exactly what you're looking for.

California

American Herbalists Guild
P.O. Box 1683
Soquel, California, 95073
Write for information regarding its classes, conferences, and newsletter.

Herb Products Company
11012 Magnolia Boulevard
North Hollywood, California 91601

Love Potions
31255 Cedar Valley Drive, Suite 317
Westlake Village, California 91362
(800) 856-8380

Mountain Rose Herbs
P.O. Box 2000
Redway, California 95560
(707) 923-7867; (800) 879-3337

Star Herb Company
38 Miller Avenue
Mill Valley, California 94941

Colorado

Cat Creek Herbs
P.O. Box 227
Florence, Colorado 81226

Green Mountain Herbs
P.O. Box 2369
Boulder, Colorado 80306

Illinois

Burgess Plant and Seed Company
2200 E. Oakland Avenue
Bloomington, Illinois 61701

The Green Earth
2545 Prairie
Evanston, Illinois 60201
(800) 322-3662

Iowa

Frontier Cooperative Herbs
3021 78th Street
Norway, Iowa 52318
(800) 669-3275

Louisiana

African Harvest
3212 Tulane Avenue
New Orleans, Louisiana 70119
(504) 822-2200

Brier Rose Herb, Inc.
8632 Highway 23
Belle Chasse, Louisiana 70037
(504) 392-7499

Maine

Swedish Herbal Institute
P.O. Box 99
York Harbor, Maine 03911
(207) 351-1084; (800) 619-1199

Maryland

St. John's Herb Garden
7711 Hillmeade Road
Bowie, Maryland 20720
(301) 262-5302; fax: (301) 262-2489

Missouri

Willow Rain Herb Farm
P.O. Box 15
Grubville, Missouri 63041

New Hampshire

Willow Keep
RR 3, N. River Road
Milford, New Hampshire 03055

New Jersey

Herbalist and Alchemist
P.O. Box 553
Broadway, New Jersey 08803
(908) 689-9020

New Mexico

Seeds of Change
P.O. Box 15700
Santa Fe, New Mexico 87506
(505) 438-8080; fax: (505) 438-7052

New York

Aphrodisia
28 Carmine Street
New York, New York 10014

Harvest Herb Company
RR 3, Box 51
Creighton Road
Malone, New York 12953
(518) 483-0030

Herbs From the Forest
P.O. Box 655
Bearsville, New York 12409

Ohio

Ohio Hempery
7002 Route 329
Guysville, Ohio 45735
(614) 662-4367; (800) 289-4367

Oregon

Atlantis Rising
7915 S.E. Stark Street
Portland, Oregon 97215

Herb Pharm
P.O. Box 116
Williams, Oregon 97544

Starflower
885 McKinley Street
Eugene, Oregon 97402

Two Dragons Trading Company
4638 S.W. Beaverton
Hillsdale Highway
Portland, Oregon 97221
(800) 896-3724

Pennsylvania

Penn Herb Company
603 N. 2nd Street
Philadelphia, Pennsylvania 19123

Rhode Island

Green Herb Garden
Green, Rhode Island 02872

South Dakota

Guerney Seed and Nursery Company
Yankton, South Dakota 57079

Vermont

Herb Closet
P.O. Box 964
Montpelier, Vermont 05602
(802) 223-0888

Northeast Herb Association
P.O. Box 146
Marshfield, Vermont 05658

Write for information regarding its classes, meetings, and newsletter. It also offers a catalog of practitioners, teachers, and herb suppliers.

Washington

Herb Technology
1305 N.E. 45th Street, Suite 205
Seattle, Washington 98105
(800) 659-2077; fax: (206) 547-4240

Hermit's Grove Herb Closet
9724 132nd Avenue N.E.
Kirkland, Washington 98033

Pan's Forest Herb Company
411 Ravens Road
Port Townsend, Washington 98368

Wisconsin

Avonlea Organic Herb Farm
Balsam Lake, Wisconsin 54810
(715) 857-5091

Canada

Herbally Yours
P.O. Box 612
Kamloops, British Columbia V2C 5L7
Canada

Wide World of Herbs, Ltd.
11 St. Catherine Street E.
Montreal, Quebec H2X 1K3
Canada

8

Magickal and
Metaphysical Shops

Where can a modern Witch go to buy dragon's blood ink, ready-made love potions, pentacle-embroidered capes, or handmade ritual tools that have been consecrated and charged with power during the correct phase of the Moon?

Wiccans, Pagans and other magickal folks have very special needs. We cannot simply walk into the local K Mart, supermarket, or religious supply store and find the items we need and want for our worship and spellcraft.

Fortunately there are special shops designed just for us and our Witchy needs. These shops are listed alphabetically by state, and contain at least the basic magick paraphernalia (books, incense, candles, ritual tools, jewelry, and so forth). Many also carry handmade and rare, one-of-a-kind items. This section also lists shops located throughout Canada, Great Britain, and Germany.

If you do not live in an area that has (or is within reasonable driving distance to) a Witchcraft supply store, or if you are still in the "broom closet" and do not want to run the risk of having friends, coworkers, or family members spot you walking out of a New Age bookstore with shopping bags overflowing with magickal merchandise, then mail order is your best bet (see Section 9). Shopping at home from a catalog is easy, discreet, and fun. (It also saves gas and keeps you from having to deal with traffic, going out in bad weather, and other inconveniences.) And like the stores, the mail order companies also offer merchandise ranging from the basic items to the most unique specialties. (Be sure to tell them you saw their listing in this book!)

Many of the shops and mail order businesses listed in the following two sections are owned and operated by practicing Pagans. They understand your needs, and if you are new to the Craft, more than likely they will be happy to offer you advice, recommend certain books and products, and even arrange for special orders (if they offer custom-made items and services).

Alabama

Ibis Books   1219-B Jordan Lane, Huntsville, Alabama 35816

Lodestar Books   2020 11th Avenue S., Birmingham, Alabama 35205

Alaska

The Source   329 E. 5th Avenue, Anchorage, Alaska 99501

Arkansas

Crazy Earl Enterprises   812 N. 32nd (Grand Plaza), Fort Smith, Arkansas 72903; phone: (501) 783-3293

Spice of Life   P.O. Box 404, Cave City, Arkansas 72521

Arizona

Alpha Book Center   1928 E. McDowell Road, Phoenix, Arizona 85006; phone: (602) 253-1223

Cosmic Art Vortex   633 N. 5th, Cottonwood, Arizona 86326

Humanspace Books   1617 N. 32nd Street, no. 5, Phoenix, Arizona 85008

Light Unlimited Bookshop   4747 E. Thomas Road, Phoenix, Arizona 85012; phone: (602) 952-8164

Magic Heart Trading Post   Box 817, Winslow, Arizona 86047

New Age Books and Gifts   6019 N. 35th Avenue, Scottsdale, Arizona 85254; phone: (602) 841-4933

The Sacred Grove   5115 N. 27th Avenue, Phoenix, Arizona 85017; phone: (602) 789-1530

California (Southern)

Akashic Record Books   1414 E. Thousand Oaks Boulevard, Thousand Oaks, California 91362

Alexandria II   3683-A Colorado Boulevard, Pasadena, California 91107

Bodhi Tree Books   8585 Melrose, Los Angeles, California 90069

Chela Bookstore   27601 Forbes, no. 37, Laguna Hills, California 92654

Chip'n Books   14181 Newport Boulevard, Tustin, California 92680

The Craft Shop   201 Moneta, Bakersfield, California 93308

Controversial Books   3021 University Avenue, San Diego, California 92104

Crystal Cave   777 S. Main Street, Suite 2, Orange, California 92668; phone: (714) 543-0551

The Crystal Cave   415 W. Foothill Boulevard, Claremont, California 91771

Desiree's Bewitchery   951 Firwood, Anaheim, California 92806

Eye of the Cat   3314 E. Broadway, Long Beach, California 90803; phone: (310) 438-3569

Feminist Wicce   21050 Waveview, Topanga, California 90290

Heart of Light Books   451 E. Ojai, Ojai, California 93023

House of Hermetic   5338 Hollywood Boulevard, Los Angeles, California 90027

Lady Bountiful   1513 Aviation Boulevard, Redondo Beach, California 90278

Magick Bookstore   2306 Highland Avenue, National City, California 92050

The Magick Circle   956 N. Lake Avenue, Pasadena, California 91104; phone: (818) 794-6013

Moon Gate Graphics   305 W. Torrance Boulevard, Carson, California 90745

Northern Mists   878 Jackman, no. 103, El Cajon, California 92020

Page One   1196 E. Walnut Street, Pasadena, California 91106; phone: (818) 798-8694; outside of California: (800) 359-8694

Panpipes Magickal Marketplace   1641 N. Cahuenga Boulevard, Hollywood, California 90028; phone: (213) 462-7078

Phoenix Bookstore   514 Santa Monica Boulevard, Santa Monica, California 90401

Psychic Eye Bookshop   13435 Ventura Boulevard, Sherman Oaks, California 91401; phone: (818) 906-8263

Psychic Eye Bookshop   21800 Ventura Boulevard, Woodland Hills, California 91364; phone: (818) 340-0033

Psychic Eye Bookshop   1011 N. Olive Avenue, Burbank, California 91502; phone: (818) 845-8831

Psychic Eye Bookshop   218 Main, Venice, California 90294; phone: (310) 396-0110

Psychic Eye Bookshop   3902 Pacific Coast Highway, Torrance, California 90505; phone: (310) 378-7754

Psychic Eye Bookshop   702 Pearl, La Jolla, California 92037; phone:
(619) 551-8877

Sorcerer's Shop   8246½ Santa Monica Boulevard, Hollywood,
California 90046

The Wizzard's Shoppe   5329 El Cajon Boulevard, San Diego,
California 92115

California (Northern)

Ancient Ways   4075 Telegraph Avenue, Oakland, California 94609;
phone: (510) 653-3244

Assembly of Wicca   4715 Franklin, Sacramento, California 95820

The Brass Unicorn   845 E. Fern, Fresno, California 93701

Cerridwen's Touch   803 Valencia, San Francisco, California 94110

Claire Light Books   1110 Petaluma Hill Road, Santa Rosa, California
95404

Creative Awareness Books   1120-C Fulton Avenue, Sacramento,
California 95825

Curios and Candles   289 Divisadero, San Francisco, California 94117

Earthspirit Books   3315 Sacramento Street, no. 525, San Francisco,
California 94118

East-West Books   1170 El Camino Real, Menlo Park, California
94025

Field's Books   1419 Polk Street, San Francisco, California 94109

Minerva's Books   1027 Alma Street, Palo Alto, California 94301

Old Wive's Tales   1009 Valencia, San Francisco, California 94110

Psychic Eye   301 Fell Street, San Francisco, California 94102; phone:
(415) 863-9997

San Jose Bookshop   1231 Kentwood, San Jose, California 95129

Sunrise Bookshop   3054 Telegraph Avenue, Berkeley, California
94705

The Sword and Rose   85 Carl Street, San Francisco, California 94117

Town and Country Books   420 Town and Country Village, San Jose, California 95128

Uma's Occult Shop   1915 Page Street, San Francisco, California 94117

Colorado

Celebration   2209 W. Colorado Avenue, Colorado Springs, Colorado 80904

Charon   230 E. 20th Avenue, Denver, Colorado 80205

Coven Gardens   P.O. Box 1064, Boulder, Colorado 80306

Crystalight Psychic Center   1562 S. Parker Road, Denver, Colorado 80231

Cultural Crossroads   3000 E. Colfax Avenue, no. 355, Denver, Colorado 80206; phone: (303) 754-2994

Faeries Garden   1060 S. Raritan, Denver, Colorado 80223

Lighthouse New Age Books   1201 Pearl, Boulder, Colorado 80302

Metaphysical Bookstore   9511 E. Colfax Avenue, Aurora, Colorado 80010

Pandora's Box   1135 N. Lincoln, no. 3, Loveland, Colorado 80537

Snowy Creek Studios   620 Main Street, Fairplay, Colorado 80440; phone: (719) 836-2050

So What?   506 5th Street, Georgetown, Colorado 80444

Connecticut

Avalon   9 N. Main Street, South Norwalk, Connecticut 06854; phone: (203) 838-5928

Curious Goods Witchcraft Shop   415 Campbell Avenue, West Haven, Connecticut 06516; phone: (203) 932-1193

Edge of the Woods Grocery　275 Edgewood, New Haven, Connecticut 06511

Gaian Goods　222 Bradley Avenue, Bldg. 8, Unit 8B, Waterbury, Connecticut 06708; phone: (203) 757-0102

Incantations　16 Ann Street, Meriden, Connecticut 06450; phone: (203) 238-9097.

Magick Mirror　243 Naugatuck Avenue, Milford, Connecticut 06460

The Wizard　425 Kings Highway East, Fairfield, Connecticut 06430; phone: (203) 367-6355

Delaware

Book Thrift　Tri-State Mall/Lower Level, I-95 and Naamans Road, Claymont, Delaware 19703

Hen's Teeth Bookstore　214 N. Market Street, Wilmington, Delaware 19801

Trinket's　2-A Baltimore Avenue, Rehoboth Beach, Delaware 19971; phone: (302) 226-2466

Florida

Athene　6851 Bird Road, Miami, Florida 33155

The Awareness Center　1003 Park Street, Jacksonville, Florida 32204; phone: (904) 353-4270

Center of Metaphysical Study　8683 Griffin, Cooper City, Florida 33328

Changing Times　911 Village Boulevard, West Palm Beach, Florida 33409; phone: (407) 640-0496

Gladstar Books　154 Cone, Ormand, Florida 32074

Jeani's Secrets New Age Bookstore　4469 S. Congress Avenue, Lake Worth, Florida 33461; phone: (407) 642-3255

Kemet House　4315 Brentwood Avenue, Jacksonville, Florida 32206; phone: (904) 356-3922

Magical Forest   2072 N. University Drive, Pembroke Pines, Florida 33024; phone; (305) 438-9399; (305) 438-9398

Magickal Forest   5725 Hollywood, Hollywood, Florida 33021

Merlin's Books   2568 E. Fowler Avenue, Tampa, Florida 33612; phone: (813) 972-1766

Metaphysical Unity Bookstore   1957 S. Flager Drive, West Palm Beach, Florida 33401; phone: (407) 833-6483

Mi-World   9808 N.W. 80th, no. 10-N, Hialeah Gardens, Florida 33016

Momma's Medica   444 Brickell, Miami, Florida 33131

Mystic Goddess Metaphysical Center   12041 66th Street N., Largo, Florida 34643; phone: (813) 530-9994

New Age Books and Things   4401 N. Federal Highway, Fort Lauderdale, Florida 33308; phone: (305) 771-0026

A Novel Thought   1227 E. Mohawk, Tampa, Florida 33604

The 9th Chakra   817 Lincoln Road, South Beach, Miami, Florida 33133; phone: (305) 538-0671

Spiral Circle   750 N. Thornton, Orlando, Florida 32803

Tomes and Treasures Books   108 N. Moody, Tampa, Florida 33609; phone: (813) 251-9368

Under the Stars   1760 N.W. 38th, Lauderhill, Florida 33311

Vortech   phone: (407) 879-0578 (Call for address and business hours.)

WHVH Psychic Bookshop   4154 Herschel Street, Jacksonville, Florida 32210; phone: (904) 387-2064

Georgia

Avalon Center   3120 Maple Street N.E., Atlanta, Georgia 30305; phone: (404) 233-1611

Phoenix and Dragon Bookstore for a New Age   300 Hammond Drive N.E., Atlanta, Georgia 30328; phone: (404) 255-5207

Shadowlight Products   2974 Hollywood, Decatur, Georgia 30033

The Sphinx   1510 Piedmont Avenue N.E., Ashley Square, Atlanta, Georgia 30324; phone: (404) 875-2665

Hawaii

Sirius Books   2320 Young, Honolulu, Hawaii 96826; phone: (808) 947-4910

Idaho

Totem   1214 E. Main Street, Burley, Idaho 83318; phone: (208) 678-4526

Illinois

Alchemy, The Eclectic Rock and Metaphysical Shop   815 Plainfield Road, Joliet, Illinois 60436; phone: (815) 722-7467

Arum Solis Books and Supplies   5113 N. Clark Street, Chicago, Illinois 60640; phone: (312) 334-2120

Back to the Source   610 E. State Street, Rockford, Illinois 61104; phone: (815) 987-0181

Explorations   934 N. Bourland, Peoria, Illinois 61606; phone: (309) 674-1242

Insight Books   505 S. First, Champaign, Illinois 61820

Isis Rising   7005 N. Glenwood Avenue, Chicago, Illinois 60657

Light of the Moon   809 Dempster Street, Evanston, Illinois 60201; phone: (708) 492-0492

Little Shop of Incense   1210 W. Granville, Chicago, Illinois 60660

Moon Mystique   614 W. Belmont Avenue, Chicago, Illinois 60657; phone: (312) 665-9016

Mystic Link Books 218 Mobileland, Bloomington, Illinois 61701

Occult Bookstore 1561 N. Milwaukee Avenue, Chicago, Illinois 60622; phone: (312) 292-0995

The Sunshine House 1504 N. 8th, Vandalia, Illinois 62471

Indiana

Astrology and Spiritual Study 4535 Hohman, Hammond, Indiana 46327

Celtic Moon Curios P.O. Box 2244, East Chicago, Indiana 46312, phone: (219) 392-3280

Eye of Osiris 111 N. Dunn, Bloomington, Indiana 47401

Midgard Runeshop Box 2022, Evansville, Indiana 47714

Silver Enterprises 206 N. 18th, Richmond, Indiana 47374

Iowa

Moon Mystique 114½ College Street, no. 16, Iowa City, Iowa 52240; phone: (319) 338-5752

Kentucky

Babylon's End Percussion 8830 E. Bend Road, Burlington, Kentucky 41005; phone: (606) 689-5275

Louisiana

Barksdale Enterprises 7877 Jefferson Highway, Baton Rouge, Louisiana 70809; phone: (504) 927-2385

Bottom of the Cup Tea Room 616 Conti Street, New Orleans, Louisiana 70130; phone: (504) 524-1997

Bottom of the Cup Tea Room and Gifts 732 Royal Street, New Orleans, Louisiana 70116; phone: (504) 523-1204

Cosmic Crystal Bookstore and Emporium   7815 Maple, New Orleans, Louisiana 70118; phone: (504) 861-3303

The Crescent Moon   736 Orleans Avenue, New Orleans, Louisiana 70116; phone: (504) 528-9400

Life's Journey Bookstore   3313 Richland Avenue, Metairie, Louisiana 70001; phone: (504) 885-2375; fax: (504) 454-5122

Marie Laveau House of Voodoo   739 Bourbon Street, New Orleans, Louisiana 70116; phone: (504) 581-3751

The Witches' Closet   521 St. Philip Street, New Orleans, Louisiana 70116; phone: (504) 593-9222

Maine

Enchantments   16 McKown Street, Boothbay Harbor, Maine 04538; phone: (207) 633-4992

Gulf of Maine Books   61 Main, Brunswick, Maine 04011

Maryland

Avante Garde Books   26 W. Susquehanna, Baltimore, Maryland 21204

Cauldron Crafts   915 Montpelier, Baltimore, Maryland 21218

Circle West Books   38 West Street, Annapolis, Maryland 21401

Concatentions   8032 Main Street, Ellicott City, Maryland 21043

Fire and Spirit Candles   36 W. 25th Street, Baltimore, Maryland 21218

Grandma's Candles Shop   113 W. Saratoga Street, Baltimore, Maryland 21201

North Door Books   4906 Berwyn, no. D, College Park, Maryland 20740

Port Market Place   1715 Eastern Avenue, Baltimore, Maryland 21231

Renaissance Books   8101 Main Street, Ellicott City, Maryland 21043; phone: (410) 465-0010; (800) 235-8097

Second Sight   903 Forest Terrace, Annapolis, Maryland
   21401

The Shaken Tree   1331-S Rockville Pike, Rockville, Maryland 20852;
   phone: (301) 217-0884

Massachusetts

Abyss   48 Chester Road, Chester, Massachusetts 01011; phone: (413)
   623-2155

Angelica of the Angels   7 Central Street, Salem, Massachusetts 01970;
   phone: (508) 745-9355

Arsenic and Old Lace   1743 Massachusetts Avenue, Cambridge,
   Massachusetts 02140; phone: (617) 354-7785

Center of Illumination   209 Main Street, Buzzards Bay,
   Massachusetts 02532; phone: (508) 759-7359

Crow Haven Corner   125 Essex Street, Salem, Massachusetts 01970

Featherstones   Twinboro Crossing Plaza, Route 20 West, Marlboro,
   Massachusetts 01752; phone: (508) 460-8048

Food for Thought   67 N. Pleasant, Amherst, Massachusetts 01002

Harc and Tortoise Bookery and Womynplace Gifts
   92 Washington Street, Fairhaven, Massachusetts 02719; phone:
   (508) 994-2408

Infinity   955 Ashley Boulevard, New Bedford, Massachusetts 02745;
   phone: (508) 995-2221

The Magic Attic   251 W. Central, no. 189, Natick, Massachusetts
   01760

The New Moon   262 Main Street, Marlboro, Massachusetts 01752;
   phone: (508) 481-7533

Of All Ages New Age Store and Cafe   289 Salem Road (Route 60),
   Medford, Massachusetts 02155; phone: (617) 391-1313; (617)
   391-3131

Open Doors Metaphysical Books and Gifts 351 Washington Street, Braintree, Massachusetts; phone: (617) 843-8224

Pyramid Books: The New Age Store 214 Derby Street, Salem, Massachusetts 01970; phone: (508) 745-7171

Shambalah Books 58 John F. Kennedy Street, Cambridge, Massachusetts 02140

Solstice Sun 10 Nason Street, Maynard, Massachusetts 01754; phone: (508) 461-0400

Tarr and Feathers 74 Federal Street, Greenfield, Massachusetts 01301; phone: (413) 733-3921; (800) 428-5126

Unicorn Books 1210 Massachusetts Avenue, Arlington, Massachusetts 02174

The Wizard's Workshop 37 Rose Street, Watertown, Massachusetts 02172

Woman of Wands Route 2 (in the River House), South Lee, Massachusetts 01260; phone: (413) 243-4036

Your Last Chance Museum Place Mall, Salem, Massachusetts 01970; phone: (508) 745-9687

Michigan

Capricorn Moon 210½ Petoskey Street, Suite A, Petoskey, Michigan 49770; phone: (616) 347-2235

Crazy Wisdom Books 206 N. 4th, Ann Arbor, Michigan 48106

Mayflower Books 2645 W. 12 Mile, Berkeley, Michigan 48072

Middle Earth Books 2791 E. 14 Mile, Sterling Heights, Michigan 48204

Middle of Nowhere Used Books W. 4213 County Road 360, Daggett, Michigan 49821; phone: (906) 753-2315

Morrigan's Incenses 10156 Maplelawn, Detroit, Michigan 48204

New Age Metaphysical Bookstore   3920 N.W. River Road, Sanford, Michigan 48657; phone: (517) 687-2271

Omni Spectrum   12083 Weiman, Hell, Michigan 48169

Roots and Wings   980 Winchester Avenue, Lincoln Park, Michigan 48146; phone: (313) 388-9141

Sacred Sparks   5071 Mount Bliss Road, East Jordan, Michigan 49727; phone: (616) 536-2704

Minnesota

Amazon Books   1612 Harmon Place, Minneapolis, Minnesota 55403

Crystals and Wolf   414 Division Street, Northfield, Minnesota 55057; phone: (507) 663-7720

Evenstar Bookstore   2401 University Avenue W., St. Paul, Minnesota 55114; phone: (612) 644-3727

Many Voices   727 Grand, St. Paul, Minnesota 55105

Mother Lode Book and Women's Center   813 W. 50th Street, Minneapolis, Minnesota 55419; phone: (612) 824-3825

New Age Bookstore   122 E. 2nd Street, Winona, Minnesota 55987; phone: (507) 454-3947

Sunsight Books   616 W. Lake Street, Minneapolis, Minnesota 55408

Symbios: Art and the Arcane   125 S.E. Main Street, no. 148, Minneapolis, Minnesota 55414; phone: (612) 331-7412

Mississippi

Lemuria Books   238 Highland Village, 4500 I-55 North, Jackson, Mississippi 39211

Missouri

The Alchemist Shop   2519 Woodson, Overland, Missouri 63114

Celestial Horizons   5337-F S. Campbell Avenue, Springfield, Missouri 65807; phone: (417) 889-9940; (800) 273-9940

Gypsie's Tea Room   Route 1, Box 23A, Carl Junction, Missouri 64834; phone: (417) 649-7982

Renaissance Books and Gifts   1337 E. Montclair, Springfield, Missouri 65807; phone: (417) 883-5161

White Light New Age Books   1687 W. 39th Street, Kansas City, Missouri 64111; phone: (816) 931-0116

Nevada

Bell, Book and Candle   1725 E. Charleston Boulevard, Las Vegas, Nevada 89104; phone: (702) 384-6807

Catz Eye   2784 E. Charleston Boulevard, Las Vegas, Nevada 89104; phone: (702) 384-3330

Ye Old Herb Doctor   125 N. Bruce, Las Vegas, Nevada 89101

New Hampshire

The Dragon's Hoard   41 Greely, Nashua, New Hampshire 03061

Isis   38 N. Main Street, Concord, New Hampshire 03301

Open Sesame Books   13 Rumford Street, Concord, New Hampshire 03301

Our Lady of Enchantment Gift Shop   39 Amherst Street, Nashua, New Hampshire 03060; phone: (603) 880-7237

Stuff n Such/The Wishful Witch   1 Stoneybrook Lane, Finch Plaza, Exeter, New Hampshire 03833; phone: (603) 778-7630

Willow Keep   RR 3, N. River Road, Milford, New Hampshire 03055

The Witchery   101 Manchester, Manchester, New Hampshire 03101

The Witches' Brew   206 Market, Portsmouth, New Hampshire 03801

New Jersey

Archaic Craft   17 Dunvale Road, Wantage, New Jersey 07461; phone: (201) 875-1321

The Equinox   108 Brighton Avenue, Long Branch, New Jersey 07740; phone: (908) 222-0801

Merchant Street Booksellers   120 W. Merchant, Audubon, New Jersey 08106

The Philosopher's Stone   557 Route 46, Kenvil, New Jersey 08106

New Mexico

Blue Eagle Book and Metaphysical Center   8334 Lomas Boulevard N.E., Albuquerque, New Mexico 87102; phone: (505) 268-3682

Brotherhood of Life Metaphysical Bookstore   110 Dartmouth S.E., Albuquerque, New Mexico 87106; phone: (505) 255-8980

Full Circle Books   2205 Silver Avenue S.E., Albuquerque, New Mexico 87106; phone: (505) 266-0022

Open Mind Metaphysical Booksellers   119 Harvard Drive S.E., Albuquerque, New Mexico 87106; phone: (505) 262-0066

New York

Bell, Book and Candle Esoterica   33 Lebanon Street, Hamilton, New York 13346; phone: (315) 824-5409

Blue White Rainbow   10 New Karner Road, Albany, New York 12203; phone: (518) 869-6915

Cosmic Vortex East   107-A The Commons, Ithaca, New York 14850

Earth Emporium   511 Ridge Road, Lackawanna, New York 14218; phone: (716) 827-0623

Eden's Garden   28 Main Street, Box 33, Freeville, New York 13068

Enchanted Candle Shoppe   2321 Westchester Avenue, Bronx, New York 10462; phone: (718) 892-5350

Enchantments, Inc. 341 E. 9th Street, New York, New York 10003; phone: (212) 228-4394

Little Turtle Trading Company 3932 58th, Woodside, New York 11377

Magickal Childe 35 W. 19th Street, New York, New York 10011; phone: (212) 242-7182

Meadowsweet Herbal Apothecary 77 E. 4th Street, New York, New York 10003; phone: (212) 254-2870; (800) 879-4161

Moon Magic 97 Main Street, Geneseo, New York 14554; phone: (716) 243-0750

New Alexandrian Books 102 The Commons, Ithaca, New York 14850

Other Worldly Waxes . . . and Whatever, Inc. 131 E. 7th Street, New York, New York 10009; phone: (212) 260-9188

Rivendell 109 Saint Mark's Place, New York, New York 10003

Rutland Road Religious Store 1043 Rutland Road, Brooklyn, New York 11212

Three of Cups 115 Tinker Street, Woodstock, New York 12498

The Wild Rose 2 Market Street, Potsdam, New York 13676; phone: (315) 265-0160

Womankind Books 5 Kivy, Huntington Station, New York 11746

Ohio

Crazy Ladies Books 4168 Hamilton Avenue, Cincinnati, Ohio 45223

Curiosity Shop 118 E. Northern Avenue, Lima, Ohio 45801; phone: (419) 222-1335

Earth Rhythm Workshop 2488 Nadine Circle, Hinckley, Ohio 44233; phone: (216) 273-6260

Enchanted Cottage 1251 S. Reynolds, no. 143, Toledo, Ohio 43615

Epic Books   232 Xenia, Yellow Springs, Ohio 45387

House of Astrology   1449 Messenger, South Euclid, Ohio 44121

Library Books   4836 Hills and Dales N.W., Jackson Township, Ohio 43030

Manifestations   31 Colonial Arcade, Cleveland, Ohio 44155

Moonstar   38422 Lake Shore Boulevard, Willoughby, Ohio 44094; phone: (216) 942-5652

New World Books   336 Ludlow, Cincinnati, Ohio 45220

The Shadow Realm   21 W. Brighton Road, Columbus, Ohio 43202, phone: (614) 262-1175

Star Spectrum   1484 Roycroft, Lakewood, Ohio 44107

Tradewinds   1652 N. High Street, Columbus, Ohio 43201

Oklahoma

Curious Goods   1319 W. Lee Boulevard, Lawton, Oklahoma 73502; phone: (405) 353-5355; (800) 256-HERB

The Four Winds   761 Asp, Norman, Oklahoma 73069

Peace of Mind   1401 E. 15th Street, Tulsa, Oklahoma 74120; phone: (800) 523-1090

Starwind   3015 Classen Boulevard, Oklahoma City, Oklahoma 73106

Oregon

Grass Roots Books   227 S.W. 2nd, Corvallis, Oregon 97333

Peralandra Books and Music   1016 Willamette Street, Eugene, Oregon 97401; phone: (503) 485-4848

Rosebud and Fish Community Bookstore   524 State Street, Salem, Oregon 97301; phone: (503) 399-9960

Woman's Place Books   2349 S.E. Ankeny, Portland, Oregon 97214

Pennsylvania

Cosmic Visions, Ltd.   956 Hamilton Street, Allentown, Pennsylvania 18102; phone: (610) 433-3610

Earth Magic   c/o Elaine's, Great Valley Shopping Center, Route 30–Lincoln Highway, North Versailles, Pennsylvania 15137

Gypsy Heaven   115 S. Main Street, New Hope, Pennsylvania 18938; phone: (215) 862-5251

Hands of Aries   620 S. 4th Street, Philadelphia, Pennsylvania 19147; phone: (215) 923-5264

Harry's Occult Shop   1238 South Street, Philadelphia, Pennsylvania 19147

Mystickal Tymes   127 S. Main Street, New Hope, Pennsylvania 18938; phone: (215) 862-5629

Perceptions Bookstore   328 W. 6th Street, Erie, Pennsylvania 16507; phone: (814) 454-7364

Sagittarius Books   87 S. Main Street, New Hope, Pennsylvania 18938

Solomon's Seal O.S.C.   9 E. Main Street, Kutztown, Pennsylvania 19530; phone: (610) 683-0822

Spider Herbs   111 Branch, Pittsburgh, Pennsylvania 15215

Rhode Island

Merlin's Closet   166 Valley, Providence, Rhode Island 02909

Metagion   184 Angell, Providence, Rhode Island 02906

Midnight Magic Curios   14 Manchester, West Warwick, Rhode Island 02893

White Light Books   562 Atwells Avenue, Providence, Rhode Island 02909

South Carolina

Psychic Shoppe   Route 2, Box 274-B, Leesville, South Carolina 29070

Stardust Books   2508 Devine Street, Columbia, South Carolina 29205; phone: (803) 771-0633

Tennessee

Maggie's Pharm   13 Florence, Memphis, Tennessee 38104

The Spider's Web   873 Par, Memphis, Tennessee 38127

The Wicca Basket   1500 Southside Avenue, Bristol, Tennessee 37620; phone: (615) 968-1313

Texas

Aquarian Age Books   5603 Chaucer, Houston, Texas 77005

Book People   4006 S. Lamar Boulevard, Suite 250, Austin, Texas 78704

Botanica Perez Drugstore   311 N. Zaramora Street, San Antonio, Texas 78207; phone: (210) 433-9001

Celebration   108 W. 43rd Street, Austin, Texas 78751; phone: (512) 453-6207

The Constellation   2829 W. Northwest Highway, Suite 846, European Crossroads, Dallas, Texas 75220; phone: (214) 352-4847

Cosmic Cup Cafe   2912 Oak Lawn Avenue, Dallas, Texas 75207; phone: (214) 521-6157

Devonshire Apothecary   2105 Ashby, Austin, Texas 78704

Flight of the Phoenix   1034 N. Carrier Parkway, Grand Prairie, Texas 75050; phone: (214) 642-6363

A Gift From the East   4701 University Oaks, Houston, Texas 77004

House of Avalon/Papa Jim Botanica   5630 S. Flores Street, San Antonio, Texas 78214; phone: (210) 922-6665

House of Power   2509 Canal Street, Houston, Texas 77003

Insight Books   14454 Midway Road, Dallas, Texas 75244; phone: (214) 661-3173

Lucia's Garden   2942 Virginia Street, Houston, Texas 77098; phone: (713) 523-6494

M Z Nita's Candle, Incense and Herb Shop   5521 E. Grand Avenue, Dallas, Texas 75223; phone: (214) 823-5471

Magick Cauldron   2214 Richmond Avenue, Houston, Texas 77098; phone: (713) 468-8031

New Age   1201 Lake Air Drive, Waco, Texas 76710

New Age Books   1006 S. Lamar Boulevard, Austin, Texas 78704

The Occult Shop   2222 Yale, Houston, Texas 77076

O.L.S.F. Metaphysical Center   5304-A Bellaire Boulevard, Bellaire, Texas 77401

Overtones Books and Gifts   14902 Preston Road at Beltline, Dallas, Texas 75240; phone: (214) 458-0404

Rosario's-Mystic   5314 Canal Street, Houston, Texas 77011

Shalimar's Mystic Shop   2633 W. Davis Street, Dallas, Texas 75211; phone: (214) 946-5064

Sweet Remembrance   107 E. Avenue E, Copperas Cove, Texas 76522; phone: (817) 542-1555

Stanley Drug Company   2819 Lyons, Houston, Texas 77020

Unlimited Thought Foundation   5525 Blanco Road, San Antonio, Texas 78212; phone: (210) 525-0693

Ye Seekers   9336 Westview, Houston, Texas 77055

Utah

Gypsy Moon Emporium   1011 E. 900 South Street, Salt Lake City, Utah 84105; phone: (801) 521-9100

Virginia

Aquarius   6653 Arlington Boulevard, Falls Church, Virginia 22042

The Monster Museum New Age Shop Route 3, Box 678, Stuart, Virginia 24171; phone: (703) 694-8226

Mystique 3130 Tidewater Drive, Norfolk, Virginia 23509

Starbound Box 210, Ruther Glen, Virginia 22546

Washington

Akasha Metaphysical Books 1124 State, Bellingham, Washington 98225

Astrology Et Al 4728 University N.E., Seattle, Washington 98115; phone: (206) 548-9128

Aum-Nee Books 25th and D, Freighthouse Square, Tacoma, Washington 98404

Dawn Horse 918 64th N.E., Seattle, Washington 98115

Earth Magic 205 E. 4th Avenue, Olympia, Washington 98501

Goddess Rising 4006 1st Avenue N.E., Seattle, Washington 98105

The Golden Age 5445 Ballard, Seattle, Washington 98107

Illusions 113 S.W. Legion, Olympia, Washington 98501

Imprint Books 917 N. 2nd Street, Tacoma, Washington 98403

Lodestar Center 11049 8th Avenue N.E., Seattle, Washington 98105; phone: (206) 548-9128

Mandala Books and Gallery 918 64th Street N.E., Seattle, Washington 98105; phone: (206) 527-2979

Mystic Rose 714 N. 34th Street, Seattle, Washington 98103; phone: (206) 547-4766

Odyssey Books 321 Main Street, Edmonds, Washington 98020; phone: (206) 672-9064

Pan's Forest Herb Company 411 Ravens Road, Pt. Townsend, Washington 98368

Passages 310 W. Champion, Bellingham, Washington 98225

Psychic Energy Center   1912 E. 72nd Street, Tacoma, Washington 98404

Quest Bookshop   717 Broadway East, Seattle, Washington 98102

The Sage   10846 N.E. 2nd Street, Bellevue, Washington 98004

Stargazer   12727 N.E. 20th Street, Bellevue, Washington 98005

Tenzing Momo and Company   93 Pike Street, Seattle, Washington 98101; phone: (206) 623-9837

Visionary Books   2203 65th Street N.E., Seattle, Washington 98115

Wortcunning   2915½ 1st Avenue (rear), Seattle, Washington 98121

Zenith Supplies   6319 Roosevelt N.E., Seattle, Washington 98115

Wisconsin

Aquarian Sun Books   6469 W. Fond du Lac, Milwaukee, Wisconsin 53218

Astrum Argentum   325 N. Plankinton Avenue, Milwaukee, Wisconsin 53203; phone: (414) 276-6966

Microcosm Books   301 W. Lakeside, Madison, Wisconsin 53715

Mimosa Community Bookstore   212 N. Henry, Madison, Wisconsin 53703; phone: (608) 256-5432

New Earth   Ishpiming Retreat Center, Box 340, Manitowish Waters, Wisconsin 54545; phone: (715) 686-2372

Of a Like Mind Store   2095 Winnebago Street, Madison, Wisconsin 53704; phone: (608) 244-0072

Prisca Magica   815 E. Johnson Street, Madison, Wisconsin 53703

Red Oak Books   610 Main Street, LaCrosse, Wisconsin 54601

Room of One's Own Bookstore   317 W. Johnson Street, Madison, Wisconsin 53703; phone: (608) 257-7888

Shakti Books   320 State Street, Madison, Wisconsin 53703; phone: (608) 255-5007

The Three Fates   1117 E. Brady Street, Milwaukee, Wisconsin 53202; phone: (414) 276-3282

Canada

Boule de Neige Bookstore   4433 St. Denis, Montreal, Quebec H2J 2L2; phone: (514) 849-0959

Le Melange Magique   1946 St. Catherine West, Montreal, Quebec H3H 1M4; phone: (514) 938-1458; fax: (514) 486-9190

Metamorphoses Books   3418-A Park Avenue, Montreal, Quebec, H2X 2H5

Moon Shadow Books   26-671 Fort, Victoria, British Columbia V8W 1GT

New Age Books for Transformational Living, Inc.   9275 Highway 48, Markham, Ontario L6E 1A1; phone: (905) 294-3771

The Occult Shop   109 Vaughan Road, Toronto, Ontario M6C 2L9; phone: (416) 787-4043

The Occult Shop   457 Somerset Street W., Ottawa, Ontario K1R 5J7; phone: (613) 231-4138

Phoenix Metaphysical Books   10202 152nd Street, Surrey, British Columbia V3R 6N7; phone: (604) 584-7684

Starfire Books   11111 81st Avenue, Edmonton, Alberta, T6G 0S6

Great Britain

Ace of Wands   128 Macklin Street, Derby, United Kingdom

Arcana   151 Fortuneswell, Portland, Dorset, United Kingdom

Atlantis Bookshop   49-A Museum Street, London, England

Craefte Supplies   33 Oldridge Road, London, England

Fate and Fortune   35 Wellington Street, Batley, West Yorkshire, England

Gothic Image   High Street, Glastonbury, Somerset, United Kingdom

Merlin's Cave   Bron-Y-Craig, Glan-Y-Wern, Talsarnau, Gwynedd County, Wales

The Mushroom   10 Heathcote Street, Nottingham, England

Occultique   73 Kettering Road, Northampton, England

Prince Elric   498 Bristol Road, Selly Oak, Birmingham, England

The Sorcerer's Apprentice   418 Burley Lodge Road, Leeds, Yorkshire, England

Germany

Merlin Mineralien, Mystik und Esoterik   Friedrich-Ebert Strasse 143, 34119 Kassel, Germany; phone: (011-49) 561-777439

9

MAIL ORDER

Abyss Distribution
48 Chester Road, Dept. WIG
Chester, Massachusetts 01011
(413) 623-2155; fax: (413) 623-2156

Free occult catalog. Over 2,400 books, plus 5,000 other ritual items. Amulets, jewelry, herbs, perfumes, incense, burners, candles, statues, and more. Magickal one-stop shopping. Retail and wholesale.

Alternatives
P.O. Box 433
Arlington Heights, Illinois 60006
(800) 357-2719

They carry thousands of products for all your magickal needs. If they don't list it, they will try to locate any item you need—just give them a call. Catalog: $3.00.

Amulets by Merlin
P.O. Box 2643
Newport News, Virginia 23609

A complete line of original design jewelry and hand engraving. Specializes in custom design work in silver, bronze, and gold for groups or individuals. Also available, a one-of-a-kind Tarot casting set, the result of thirteen years of research. This set encompasses the Tarot, Qabalistic, and astrological correlation in each amulet, resulting in a revolutionary form of divination. Catalog: $1.00.

Ancient Circles/Open Circle
P.O. Box 610
Laytonville, California 95451
(800) 726-8032

Symbolic jewelry of Celtic design, pendants in Goddess and God images, temple formula perfumes, and exclusive "new classics" such as the Celtic Pentagram, Bamburg Green Man, and more. Catalog: $2.00.

Annwyn Tradesman
P.O. Box 321
Atco, New Jersey 08004

Finely crafted New Age tools, ornaments, and works of art. Current catalog price: $2.50 (includes a free rune sample.)

Arachne's Web
P.O. Box 4123
Virginia Beach, Virginia 23454
(804) 422-8172

Handcrafted Witchy items, including cloaks, pouches, runes, wands, jewelry, Tarot, books, and more. Catalog: $2.00 (credited to your first order).

Archaic Craft
17 Dunvale Road
Wantage, New Jersey 07461

Personalized ritual knives, staffs, wands, runes and goblets. Catalog: $2.00.

Ars Obscura
P.O. Box 20695
Seattle, Washington 98102
(206) 324-9792

Publisher of occult classical visual art, reproductions of engravings and woodcuts to poster format, grimoires, occasional ritual knives and daggers. Catalog: $2.00.

Aunt Agatha's Occult Emporium
P.O. Box 64043
RPO Clark Road
Coquitlam, British Columbia V3J 7V6
Canada
fax: (604) 931-3874

Write or fax for a free catalog of magickal items and novelties.

The Bead Tree
P.O. Box 682
West Falmouth, Massachusetts 02574
(508) 548-4665

Earrings and pendants taken from ancient images of the Goddess. Medicine card earrings and pendants with your totem animal and other charms. All contain symbols of Earth, Air, Fire, and Water. Send $1.00 for brochures.

Bell, Book and Candle
5886 Rocky Point
Long Island, New York 11778

Candles, oils, incense, herbs, sachets, pyramids, Tarot cards, Voodoo dolls, books, tapes, and more. Free catalog.

Bell, Book and Candle
2505 W. Berry Street
Fort Worth, Texas 76109

Celtic catalog. Hundreds of books, cassettes, compact discs, and jewelry. Catalog: $1.00 (refundable with first order).

Blue Earth Dream Trading Co.
8215 S.E. 13th Avenue
Portland, Oregon 97202
(503) 231-1146

Shamanistic-oriented tools, smudging herbs, crystals, feathers, Tibetan bowls, lunar and animal totems, and other items. Catalog: $2.00.

The Brass Unicorn
    845 E. Fern
    Fresno, California 93728
    (209) 441-7107

Books, incense, herbs, jewelry, art, crystals, ritual accessories, New Age music, and more.

Capestries
    Box 549
    Appleton, Maine 04862

Specializes in hats and capes. "Fun, functional, flowing, soft, and sensual." Catalog: $1.00.

Celestial Sights and Sounds, Inc.
    P.O. Box 195
    Sayville, New York 11782

A variety of Priestess designs on T-shirts, notecards, and ebony plaques. Send $10.00 for catalog (includes eight Egyptian notecards by Thor and four Priestess notecards).

Celtic Folkworks
    RD no. 4, Box 210
    Willow Grove Road
    Newfield, New Jersey 08344

Celtic Folkworks is a family-run business specializing in traditional Celtic design handcrafts and jewelry. Catalog: $1.00.

Cere's Garden
    Route 3, Box 305
    Alvin, Texas 77511

Feminist Witchcraft accessories: silk altar cloths, Tarot wraps and spread cloths, velvet Tarot, amulet and crystal bags embroidered in gold and silver with symbols of the Goddess. Herb-filled dream pillows, custom-made necklaces for healing purposes, and more. Catalog: $1.00.

Church of Universal Forces
    P.O. Box 03195
    Columbus, Ohio 43203
    (614) 252-2083

Magickal, ritual, and occult supplies. Catalog: $5.00.

The Conjured Night
P.O. Box 16844
Chapel Hill, North Carolina 27516

Witchy crafts for rituals, altars, Full Moons, celebrations, Moon-bloods, dreaming ... for the Wise One, gods or goddesses, lovers, nymphs, fairies, healers, maids, mamas, crones, consorts, and the wild night's creature in us all! Catalog: $1.00 (credited to your first order).

Cosmic Corner
Box 499
Deerfield Beach, Florida 33443
Catalog: $2.00.

Cosmic Vision, Ltd. (formerly The Occult Emporium)
956 Hamilton Street
Allentown, Pennsylvania 18102
(610) 433-3610

Ancient Wisdom Archive and Supply—retail and illustrated mail order catalog: $2.00. Books, herbs, incense, jewelry, minerals, candles, altar attire and equipment, brasses, Tarot, consultations, magick-on-contract, experts in right and left traditions. Oils, powders, antiques, arcane specialties. UFO museum on premises. Open Monday to Friday, 11 A.M. to 6 P.M., Saturday 11 A.M. to 5 P.M. Since 1975.

Coven Gardens
P.O. Box 1064
Boulder, Colorado 80306
(303) 444-4322

Occult supplies: incense, oils, bath products, herbs, candles, and more. Western Traditional ancient recipes, also Wiccan, Druidic/Celtic, Egyptian, Greco-Roman, Middle and Near Eastern, Macumba, and Voodoo (upon request). All planetary and Zodiacal blends are Qabalistic. Supplies to aid practitioners from Paganism to High Ceremonial ritual work. All products are made by planetary placements, lunar cycle phase, and during ritual circle.

Crescent Moongoddess
P.O. Box 153
Massapequa Park, New York 11762

Magick supplies for Wiccans. Send $2.00 for a nineteen-page catalog (refundable with first purchase). Make checks and money orders payable to Bonnie Thompson.

The Crystal Moon
Box 802
Matteson, Illinois 60443

Send $3.00 (refundable with first purchase) for their catalog of astrology and occult supplies.

Crystal Moon Curio Shoppe
72 Van Reipen Avenue, Suite 11
Jersey City, New Jersey 07306

Witch supplies, including books, spell kits, herbs, oils, incense, Tarot cards, mojo bags, candles, amulets, and talismans. Catalog: $2.00.

The Crystal Portal
P.O. Box 1934
Upper Marlboro, Maryland 20773
(301) 952-9470

Music, videos, jewelry, Tarot, craft supplies, magick accessories, and more. Free shipping on all orders of $25.00 or more. Free catalog.

The Crystal Rose
P.O. Box 8416
Minneapolis, Minnesota 55408
(612) 488-3715

Hand-wrapped crystal pendants, gemstone jewelry, magick wands with spell scrolls, amulet bags, runestones, New Age stationery, and much more. Send a self-addressed stamped envelope to receive a free catalog.

Curious Goods Witchcraft Shoppe
415 Campbell Avenue
West Haven, Connecticut 06516

Offers handmade magickal crystal gemstone charms for those seeking love, money, healing, or protection. Catalog: $2.00; newsletter: $2.00.

Dragons of the Heart Designs
P.O. Box 367
Snowflake, Arizona 85937
(800) 439-2638

"Awaken the Goddess within you. Art cards and sterling jewelry that captures the essence of the Goddess within in Her Maiden, Mother, and Crone aspects." Free color catalog of a complete line of cards and jewelry. Wholesale inquiries welcome.

Earthlore
1442 "A" Walnut, no. 53-W
Berkeley, California 94709

Send $2.00 for an illustrated catalog of sea wands, moon bags, elf-crystals, Tarot and pentacle pouches, medicine bags, and cloaks.

Earth Magic Productions
2166 Broadway
New York, New York 10024
(800) 662-8634

Write or call for a free catalog.

Enchantments
341 E. 9th Street
New York, New York 10003
(212) 228-4394

Witchcraft supply store and catalog. Herbs, Shaman goods, chalices, daggers, incense, books, crystal balls, oils, candles, Tarot cards, Wiccan study groups, lectures, classes, and workshops. Tarot and astrology readings by appointment. Catalog: $2.00.

The Excelsior Incense Works
P.O. Box 853
San Francisco, California 94101
(415) 822-9124

Incense from around the world, religious statues from India, raw materials to make incense, crystals, candles, and many gift items. Catalog: $1.00.

Eye of the Day
P.O. Box 21261
Boulder, Colorado 80308

"A circle of prosperity." For a free retail catalog of quality products at reasonable prices, write or call: (800) 717-3307.

Eye of the Goddess
P.O. Box 2507
Chula Vista, California 91912

Handmade metaphysical gifts and supplies. Catalog: $1.00.

Feng Shui Warehouse
(800) 399-1599

Call for a free catalog of Feng Shui products: mirrors, chimes, flutes, compasses, books, and tapes.

The Formulary
P.O. Box 5455
Grants Pass, Oregon 97527

Astrologically-correct incense, bath salts, oils, candles, books, jewelry, and many other occult supplies. Catalog: $2.50.

Gary's Gem Garden
404 Route 70 East
Cherry Hill, New Jersey 08034

Quartz crystals, hundreds of polished stones and mineral specimens from amber to zircon, books, charts, and pouches. Send a self-addressed stamped envelope for a free catalog (outside of the United States, send $1.00).

Gemstone Crafts
P.O. Box 621165
Littleton, Colorado 80167

They offer sacred and mystical gemstones and gemstone gifts. Write for more information.

Golden Isis
P.O. Box 525
Fort Covington, New York 12937

Wiccan books (including *Circle of Shadows,* by Gerina Dunwich), natal charts, spellcasting services, Tarot card readings, and more. Send a self-addressed stamped envelope for a free information package.

Grand Adventure
RD-6, Box 6198
Stroudsburg, Pennsylvania 18360

Handmade Goddess statuettes of artstone. Make your own selection among the powerful images of the goddesses that have evolved over twenty-five thousand years. Catalog: $1.00.

Gray Mouse Medicine Bag Co.
2717 Sudderth Drive
Ruidoso, New Mexico 88345
(505) 257-2717

Medicine bags, crystals, cassette tapes, bead works, fetishes, books, incense, and more. Catalog: $2.00.

Gypsy Heaven
115 S. Main Street
New Hope, Pennsylvania 18938
(215) 862-5251

"The Witch Shop of New Hope!" Specializing in books, herbs, oils, incense, and much more. Catalog: $3.00 (refundable with first purchase.)

Gypsy Moon
1780 Massachusetts Avenue, Dept. GI
Cambridge, Massachusetts 02140

"Our clothes exist for special people who feel as though they were born to another age. Our styles are transformative, designed to flow as you move. Clothing that is magic you can take with you into the larger world where magic is sorely lacking." Catalog: $2.00.

Halloran Software
P.O. Box 75713
Los Angeles, California 90075

Astrology software for IBM, PC, both DOS and Windows. For both the professional and the hobbyist. For a free catalog, write to the above address or call (800) SEA-GOAT (California residents call: (818) 501-6515).

Hamilton
    Box 1258
    Moorpark, California 93021
    Books, crystals, talismans, herbs, essential oils, incense, Tarot, videos, candles, robes, and more. Catalog: $3.00.

Harmony Ministries
    Box 1568
    Overgaard, Arizona 85933
    "Personalized musical healing tapes for your mind, body, and soul." Write for more information.

Hourglass Creations
    492 Breckenridge Street
    Buffalo, New York 14213
    Earth-friendly herbal products: soaps, oils, incense, creams, and others. Psychic readings, author-signed books, and lectures and workshops coordinated by Trish Telesco. Affiliated with MAGIC (Metaphysical Artists for Gaia) and their newsletter, *Abracadabra*. To receive a free catalog, send a self-addressed stamped envelope along with two first-class stamps.

Hypno Vision Occult Shop
    Box 2192
    Halesite, New York 11743
    Over three thousand New Age and self-help titles. Custom-made subliminal tapes upon request. Large selection of King Solomon's amulets, talismans, and pentacles, crystal balls, jewelry, and many more great magickal things. Sixty-five page brochure: $3.00 (refundable with first order).

Infinity
    955 Ashley Boulevard
    New Bedford, Massachusetts 02745
    (508) 995-2221
    Offers metaphysical books, Craft supplies, gifts, workshops, and readings. Please write or call for a catalog.

International Guild of Occult Sciences Research Society
255 El Cielo Road, Suite X565X
Palm Springs, California 92262
(619) 327-7355

Huge catalog of rare books, courses, products, psionic helmets and boxes, Witchcraft Radionics, time travel, hidden technology, alchemical money boxes, exorcism, PSI warfare, and invisibility. Teacher, researcher, or publisher memberships available. Bimonthly magazine and more. Complete information and catalog: $3.00.

Isis
5701 E. Colfax Avenue
Denver, Colorado 80220
(303) 321-0867

Metaphysical New Age center, candles, books, incense, herbs, jewelry, tapes, crystals, stone pendulums, artwork, and more. Catalog: $3.00.

Isle of Avalon

For a free catalogue of magickal goods, mystical oils, and incense, call (800) 700-ISLE (California residents, please call: (714) 646-4213).

J. L. Enterprises
P.O. Box 1069
Lakewood, California 90714

Spiritual, New Age, and American Indian items, spell kits for love, money, success, and more; oils, incenses, candles, books, runes, and Tarot cards. Catalog: $3.00.

Jane Iris Designs
P.O. Box 608
Graton, California 95444

Images of empowerment, guidance, protection, and self-expression. Jewelry, pendulums, sculpture, and candles from Jane Iris Designs, Inc. Free catalog.

Joan Teresa Power Products
P.O. Box 442
Mars Hill, North Carolina 28754
(704) 689-5739

Large selection of hard-to-find herbs and roots. Some plants available, shipped live from their nursery. Herbs, handmade fine quality oils, incense, powders and bath items, candles, books, jewelry, and more. Written lessons and personal instruction. Ten percent discount on all Wiccan products. Catalog: $2.00.

KLW Enterprises
3790 El Camino Real, no. 270
Palo Alto, California 94306

Unique designs: "Born Again Pagan" and "Howl at the Moon" buttons, bumper stickers, 8"-diameter, iron-on transfers. Catalog: $1.00.

Lea's Light
P.O. Box 33272
Charlotte, North Carolina 28233

Handmade candles—over twenty-five shapes to choose from, plus unlimited colors. Design your own. For more information, send $1.00 or a self-addressed stamped envelope.

Llethtovar Creations
P.O. Box 855
Urbana, Ohio 43078

Images of the archetypal Earth Mother and Her Priestess, hand-carved in various types of stone and available in many styles and sizes. Rainbow necklaces, Minoan breast beads, and amulet bags. Catalog: $1.00.

Llewellyn's New Worlds of Mind and Spirit

New book excerpts, readers' forum, horoscopes, weather and earthquake forecasts, New Age marketplace, and more. For a free issue, call: (800) THE-MOON.

Lunatrix
P.O. Box 800482
Santa Clarita, California 91380

Free mail order catalog featuring ritual items, Goddess jewelry, T-shirts, incense, oils, herbs, rubber stamps, and more. Please send a self-addressed stamped envelope.

The Magic Attic
251 W. Central Street, no. 189
Natick, Massachusetts 01760
Handmade Wiccan products, ritual incense, scented oils, Tarot cards, botanicals, unusual Pagan gifts, dream pillows, potpourri, handcrafted candles, ritual kits, incense burners, and much more. Catalog: $2.00.

Magickal Childe (formerly The Warlock Shop)
35 W. 19th Street
New York, New York 10011
(212) 242 7182
Witchcraft and occult supplies. Free catalog.

Magickal Creations
1024 McClendon Street
Irving, Texas 75061
(214) 438-2072
Runeboards, incense, oils, scrying mirrors, robes, wands, banners, and more. Retail or wholesale catalog: $3.00.

The Magickal Mind
P.O. Box 3737
South Pasadena, California 91030
(818) 282-7255
Incense, oils, candles, tools for divination and psychological development, books, handmade jewelry, crystals, and more. Catalog: $2.00.

Magickal Unicorn Messenger
P.O. Box 1302
Findlay, Ohio 45839
For a catalog of Pagan products, send $2.00.

Magus Books and Herbs
1316 S.E. 4th Street
Minneapolis, Minnesota 55414
(612) 379-7669
Order line: (800) 99-MAGUS. To order by computer modem, call: MAGUS BBS (612) 627-9029. Occult books, incense, oils, and supplies. Catalog: $2.00.

Marah
P.O. Box 948
Madison, New Jersey 07940

Learn magickal herbalism and make incenses to enhance your rituals with Marah's *The Magic of Herbs*, $29.95 postpaid. Full line of Wiccan herbs also available, plus flower oils, handcrafted incense, candles, books, Wicca course, and other enchantments. Send $1.00 for catalog, incense sample, and a free issue of *Marah's Almanac.*

Metatools
Box 8027
Santruce, Puerto Rico 00910

Metaphysical software for IBM and compatibles. "Great selection and prices." Free catalog.

Moondance
P.O. Box 593
Varysburg, New York 14167

Twenty-one varieties of fragrant stick incense, forty-eight kinds of oils, handmade earthenware incense burners, and other items of interest to magickal folk. Catalog: $1.00.

Moonscents and Magickal Blends
P.O. Box 381588
Cambridge, Massachusetts 02238
(800) 368-7417

Incense and oils, books, Tarot, capes, robes, herbs, jewelry, crystals, cauldrons, and more. Call or write for a free full-color magickal catalog.

Moonstar Psychic and Spiritual Center
38422 Lake Shore Boulevard
Willoughby, Ohio 44094
(216) 942-5652

Candles, books, cards, incense, tapes, herbs, oils, powders, jewelry, crystal balls, and more. Catalog: $2.00.

Mother's Magick
P.O. Box 82174
Portland, Oregon 97282

Over seventy-five essential oils, books, athames, stained glass, incense, brooms, smudging fans, herbs, powders, and more. Catalog: $1.75 (refundable with first order).

Mysteria Products
   P.O. Box 1147
   Arlington, Texas 76004

"We have something for everybody"—crystals, books, herbs, incense, jewelry, oils, candles, spell kits, stones, and talismans. Free catalog.

Mysteries
   9 Monmouth Street
   London, WC2
   England
   Phone: 01-240-3688

The largest store in the United Kingdom stocking New Age and occult books and products. Free catalog.

Mystic Arts
   105D Town Square, Suite 47
   Copperas Cove, Texas 76522

Books, incense, magick tools, and much more. Catalog: $2.00.

Mystical Essence
   P.O. Box 169
   Kearny, New Jersey 07032
   (201) 991-5388

Books, Tarot cards, oils, herbs, tapes, handmade incenses, buttons, and more. Ask about their first-time order specials. Ninety-page catalog: $2.00 (refundable with first order).

Mystical Swan Products
   Goldfox, Inc.
   P.O. Box 726
   Forest, Virginia 24551

A small New Age company dedicated to serving the Wiccan, Pagan, and eclectic occult communities. Specializes in herbal, instructional, and ritual-oriented supplies and products. Thousands to choose from. Catalog: $2.00 (discounted from first order).

Mythic Images Altar Figurines
P.O. Box 982
Ukiah, California 95482
(707) 485-7787

Exquisite sculptures of goddesses and gods, both museum-quality replicas and original interpretations. Created by Oberon and Morning Glory Zell. Send a self-addressed stamped envelope to receive a free catalog.

Nemeton
P.O. Box 1542
Ukiah, California 95482
(707) 463-1432

Books, tapes, and songbooks (especially the music of Gwydion Pendderwen), videos, and more. Publishing arm of the Church of All Worlds. Send a self-addressed stamped envelope to receive a free catalog.

The Northern Light
P.O. Box 130
Kattskill Bay, New York 12804

Books, incense, stones, jewelry, and more. Catalog: $1.00.

Nuit Unlimited
249 N. Brand Boulevard, no. 482
Glendale, California 91203
(213) 258-5734

Abundance of magickally charged, sensual, and practical products honoring all paths of ceremonial and personal work are offered in this informative, unique mail order catalog. Oils from A to Z; stick and powder incense; massage oil blends; bath salts; formulations for Wiccan, Qabalistic, and special purposes; ceremonial, meditation, and tantric tapes; statuary; books, and robes. All with total personal service and love of the Goddess. Send $3.00 for a catalog and oil or incense of your choice.

Occult Bookstore
1561 N. Milwaukee Avenue
Chicago, Illinois 60622
(312) 292-0995

Specialists in metaphysics, featuring a large selection of books on all spiritual traditions, Tarot cards, symbolic jewelry, oils, incense, stones, herbs, posters, statues, and curios. They also buy used books.

Our Lady of Enchantment/Eden Within
P.O. Box 667
Jamestown, New York 14702

"A catalog for all your magickal needs: ritual tools, candles, oils, books, herbs, robes, talismans, and much more." Catalog: $2.00 (refundable with first order).

Panpipes Magickal Marketplace
1641 N. Cahuenga Boulevard (or Box 1352)
Hollywood, California 90028
(213) 462-7078

Complete line of occult supplies, handmade robes, Tarot pouches, jewelry, books, crystals, hand-blended incense and oils, and more. Tarot, palmistry, and numerology readings given on premises. Catalog: $5.00.

Pan's Forest Herb Co.
411 Ravens Road
Port Townsend, Washington 98368

Offers Tarot decks, unique books, and bulk herbal tinctures. Free catalog.

Pan's Grove Catalogue and Newsletter
P.O. Box 124838
San Diego, California 92112

Send $1.80 for information.

Paul Beyerl
9724 132nd Avenue N.E.
Kirkland, Washington 98033

Noted herbalist and astrologer offers books, tapes, and study materials. Send $2.00 for a sample of *Hermit's Lantern*.

POTO (Procurer of the Obscure)
11002 Massachusetts Avenue
Westwood, California 90025

"A mail-order and networking company serving the new seeker and scholar as well." Herbs, jewelry, gifts, tools, and books from Abracadabra to Zen. Catalog: $5.00.

Pyramid Books and the New Age Collection
P.O. Box 48
35 Congress Street
Salem, Massachusetts 01970
(508) 744-6261 (Monday through Saturday, 10 A.M. to 5 P.M. Eastern Standard Time)

For a copy of their current catalog, send $1.00.

Rosewynd's Simples
453 Proctor Road
Manchester, New Hampshire 03109

Oils and incense for ritual and magickal use. Also has handcrafted wood amulets, runes, bath salts, wands, and other magickal items as they become available. Nearly everything in the catalog is made by Rosewynd or other Witches personally known to her. Please include a large self-addressed stamped envelope when requesting a catalog.

Rothschild-Berlin
2250 E. Tropicana, Suite 19
Las Vegas, Nevada 89119
(702) 795-1902

A collector's catalog of weird things, mysterious relics, and bizarre artifacts, plus hundreds of hard-to-find occult titles for collectors. Catalog: $5.00.

Runa-Raven
P.O. Box 557
Smithville, Texas 78957

Send $1.00 for a catalog of runic and magickal books, Norse and Germanic jewelry (including a wide selection of Thor's hammers), compact discs, audio- and videotapes, rune-staves, and other magickal tools.

Runes and Bindrunes
P.O. Box 364
Dania, Florida 33004

Handcrafted sterling silver charms, earrings, pendants, pins and custom designs. Send a self-addressed stamped envelope to receive a free catalog.

Sacred Rose
P.O. Box 331389
Fort Worth, Texas 76163
Magickal jewelry, sacred oils, spiritual stones, and powerful talismans. Free catalog.

The Sage Garden
P.O. Box 144
Payette, Idaho 83661
(208) 454-2026
Herbs, common and hard-to-find essential oils, spell kits, amulets, talismans, garb, statuary, runes, unique anointing oils, filler-free incense, bath and beauty items, and jewelry. Publisher of WPPA member publication *Artemosia's Magick!* Other services include Tarot readings and custom orders. Free catalog with large self-addressed stamped envelope and three first-class stamps.

Salamander Armoury
15258 Lakeside Street
Sylmar, California 91342
(818) 362-5339
Hand-forged athames, swords, and other ritual tools fashioned to lunar cycles. Send a self-addressed stamped envelope to receive a free catalog.

Serpentine Music Productions
P.O. Box 2564
Sebastopol, California 95473
(707) 823-7425; fax: (707) 823-6444
Hard-to-find Pagan music. Inquire about its volume discount program for religious groups. Catalog: $1.00.

Seven Sisters of New Orleans
12265 Foothill Boulevard, no. 17
Sylmar, California 91342
(818) 834-8383

The "leading manufacturer of spiritual oils, incense, bath and wash products." They also carry candles, perfumes, books, crystal balls, herbs, mojo bags, prayer cards, spell kits, statues, Tarot cards and Voodoo dolls. All orders are shipped within twenty-four hours. A free gift is sent with each order. (The value of the gift increases as the amount of your order increases.) Catalog: $2.00.

Shadow Enterprises
P.O. Box 18094
Columbus, Ohio 43218
(614) 262-1175

Offers a unique collection of one-of-a-kind items, fine metaphysical supplies, ritual tools, and jewelry; new, used and rare books; collectibles, book search service, and much more. For more information, send $1.00.

Shadow's Grove
P.O. Box 177
Cedar Creek, Texas 78612

Gemstone wands, Goddess goblets, calendars, incense, herbs, cauldrons, oils, handcrafted tree spirit brooms, prayer staffs, and more. Catalog: $5.00 (refundable with your first order).

Shapers of Fantasy
P.O. Box 5294
North Hollywood, California 91616

Carries such items as magickal mushroom folk, Sun and Moon wind chimes, Green Man wall tiles, ancient archetypes and totems, and Horned One pins and pendants. Free catalog.

Shell's Mystical Oils
P.O. Box 691646
Stockton, California 95269

Carries over three hundred different herbs, some of which are very hard to find, also occult oils, incense, tinctures, candles, altar covers, stones, charms, bags, sprinkling powders, made-to-order full-length ritual robes and capes, and much more. Catalog: $2.00.

Sidda
P.O. Box 186
Blue River, Oregon 97413

Obsidian athames, ceremonial blades, antler or obsidian herb knives, and obsidian mirrors. Send $1.00 for their brochure.

Sisters of the Moon
P.O. Box 1341
Newport Beach, California 92663

"Magickal accoutrements available for the discerning Witch. All lovingly Kitchen-Witch crafted just like Grandma use to make." Limited edition candles, clothes, oils, and more. Wholesale available. Catalog: $4.00.

Soft Touch
Box 213, Dept. RC
Bryn Mawr, California 92318

Custom candles. You choose size and shape, color and scent. Over one thousand geometric, ritual, figurine, and decorative candles. More than 125 scents (or request one of your own) and almost any color. Occult candles (knob/wishing, Witch, skulls, crosses, etc.) plus candle-burning supplies. Catalog: $2.00 (applied to first order).

Solomon Seal Occult Service Co.
9 E. Main Street
Kutztown, Pennsylvania 19530
(610) 433-3610

Occult books and supplies. Catalog: $2.00.

The Sorcerer's Apprentice
2103 Adderbury Circle
Madison, Wisconsin 53711
(608) 271-7591

Pagan robes, altar cloths, gemstones, silver pentagrams, tapes, compact discs, oils, powders, and much more. Wholesale inquiries welcome. Free catalog.

The Source
Box 484
Warrington, Pennsylvania 18976

Send $3.00 for a two hundred-page psychic directory and New Age product catalog (refundable with your first order).

Southworth Enterprises
P.O. Box 440624
Aurora, Colorado 80044
(303) 888-5667

Celtic jewelry catalog: $3.00 (refundable with your first order).

Technicians of the Sacred
1317 N. San Fernando Way, Suite 310
Burbank, California 91504

Books, music, oils, and ritual supplies related to Neo-African systems, Voudoun, and ritual magick. Catalog: $5.00.

Touch Stone
1601-A Page Street
San Francisco, California 94117
(415) 621-2782

Candles, crystals, ritual oils, altar goods, books, incense, and other occult items. Catalog: $2.00.

The Unicorn Forge
105 Crescent Street
Mazomanie, Wisconsin 53560

Knives and swords, all manner of metalwork, positive path *only*. Write for prices, giving specifics, including sketches with dimensions, if known. All edged tools are forged. All pieces warranteed against defects in materials and workmanship and cleansed prior to shipping to give the owner the purest receptacle for charging their needs.

White Light Pentacles/Sacred Spirit Products
P.O. Box 8163
Salem, Massachusetts 01971

This company is dedicated to the propagation of the Wiccan arts and magickal sciences. They are the distributors of thousands of authentic spiritual tools, talismans, jewelry, and supplies, plus many other offerings for the celebration of life. Cast a mighty spell in your home or office! Catalog: $3.00.

Widening Horizons
21713-B N.E. 141st Street
Woodinville, Washington 98072
(206) 869-9810; fax: (206) 869-1821

A complete line of numerology software. Call or write for a free catalog and samples.

Willow Keep
P.O. Box 664
Wilton, New Hampshire 03086
(603) 672-0229

Herbs, pathworking tapes, Pagan T-shirts, incense, natural wands, dolls, altar statues, bronze pentacles, and more. Also workshops and open rituals. Catalog: $1.00 (refundable with your first order.)

Woman of Wands
P.O. Box 330
South Lee, Massachusetts 01260
Phone/fax: (413) 243-4036

Specializing in Goddess religion, women's health, and Wicca. Catalog: $3.00 (credited on your first order).

Worldwide Curio House
P.O. Box 17095-G
Minneapolis, Minnesota 55417

The "world's largest Occult, Mystic Arts supply house." Thousands of curios, books, herbs, oils, gifts, unique jewelry, and talismans. Items from all over the world. Catalog: $1.00.

Wren Faire Designs
4290 Pepper Drive
San Diego, California 92105
(619) 282-2889

A small catalogue of jewelry designs, including custom silver crowns and handfasting rings.

Zephyr Services
1900 Murray Avenue
Pittsburgh, Pennsylvania 15217
(800) 533-6666; (412) 422-6600

Write or call for a free catalog of New Age software.

10

PAGAN POTPOURRI

This section contains a little of this and a little of that, but all are important to the Pagan, Wiccan, and New Age community, serving it in one way or another. You will find listings for many talented craftspeople and artists, psychic readers and counselors, computer bulletin boards, spiritual retreat centers, museums, and other persons, places, and things that could not be listed in any of the previous sections of this book.

California

Heart Art
12006 Maxwellton Road
Studio City, California 91604

Goddess greeting cards, made to order, or you can choose from a variety of hand-painted floral designs and line art.

Sacred Women's Journeys
P.O. Box 5544
Berkeley, California 94705
(510) 525-4847

Offers group tours and cruises to exotic faraway places, chanting, and Goddess rituals. For spiritually-minded women.

Colorado

Colorado Women's Center for the Performing and Visual Arts
P.O. Box 142
Fairplay, Colorado 80440
(719) 836-2177
A Pagan center providing cultural and spiritual retreats for women.

Florida

Pagan's Way
P.O. Box 5442
Hollywood, Florida 33083
(305) 925-1620; (305) 925-8403
A Pagan computer network.

Louisiana

New Orleans Voodoo Museum
724 Dumaine Street
New Orleans, Louisiana 70130
(504) 523-7685; (504) 522-5223
Open seven days a week, 10 A.M. to 6 P.M. General admission: $5.25.

Maine

Venus Adventures
P.O. Box 167
Peaks Island, Maine 04108
(207) 766-5655

Goddess tours (small groups) for fun, education, and inspiration. Call or write for additional information and tour destinations and prices.

Massachusetts

Rajj
P.O. Box 204
Monument Beach, Massachusetts 02553

Dream empowerment through Rajj. Inspirational channeling in response to individual dreams. Rajj, channeled, is close to the dream-realm, giving dynamic responses, sharing valuable insights, revealing dream's natural creative power. Send dream, questions, and check ($25.00 per dream) to Rajj.

Rebecca Nurse Homestead
149 Pine Street
Danvers, Massachusetts 01923
(508) 774-8799

The historic homestead of Rebecca Nurse (who was hanged as a Witch in 1692 on Salem's Gallows Hill). Guided tours and a twenty-five-minute slide show on the historic "Witch hysteria of 1692." Adult admission: $3.50; children under sixteen: $1.50. Open approximately June through late October. Hours: 1:00 P.M. to 4:30 P.M. Closed Mondays.

Salem Wax Museum of Witches and Seafarers
288 Derby Street
Salem, Massachusetts 01970
(508) 740-2929

Hours: September through May (10 A.M. to 5 P.M.); June through August (10 A.M. to 7 P.M.). Adult admission: $4.00; seniors: $3.50; children: $2.50.

Salem Witch Museum
192 Washington Square
Salem, Massachusetts 01970
(508) 744-1692

Offers a complete look at the Salem Witch Trials that took place in 1692. Open daily, year round. Hours: September through June (10 A.M. to 5 P.M.); July through August (10 A.M. to 7 P.M.). Adult admission: $4.00; seniors: $3.50; children six to fourteen years old: $2.50. Group rates available.

Witch Dungeon Museum
16 Lynde Street
Salem, Massachusetts 01970
(508) 741-3570

A presentation of a Witch trial adapted from the 1692 historical transcripts, reenacted by professional actors. Open daily from 10 A.M. to 5 P.M. Adult admission: $4.00; seniors: $3.50; children: $2.50.

Witch House
310½ Essex Street
Salem, Massachusetts 01970
(508) 744-0180

The restored home (circa 1642) of Jonathan Corwin, one of the Salem Witch Trials' infamous judges. Preliminary examinations of women and men accused of the crime of Witchcraft took place over three hundred years ago in this building. Open from March 15 through June 30, and Labor Day through December 1. House: 10:00 A.M. to 4:30 P.M. Adult admission: $5.00; children five to sixteen years old: $1.50.

Minnesota

International Druid Archival Deposit
Address: Carleton Archives (re: Druids)
Carleton College
Northfield, Minnesota 55057
(507) 663-4270

Founded in 1963 and open to visitors, Monday through Friday, 9 A.M. to 5 P.M. Directors: Eric Hilleman and Michael Scharding, college archivists.

Missouri

Diana's Grove
P.O. Box 159
Salem, Missouri 65560
(314) 689-2400

A retreat center on 102 wooded acres with a hot tub, swimming hole, and trails. Holds Pagan gatherings. Open to visitors by appointment only.

Gaea Retreat Center
   P.O. Box 10442
   Kansas City, Missouri 64171
   (816) 561-6111

   Located on 168 acres, this is an interfaith network center owned by Earth Rising, Inc., and open to all life-affirming traditions. Includes a dining hall, open-air pavilion, nine cabins, and a large circle area. By reservation only. Call or write for rental rates.

Goddess Wares
   4128 Holmes Boulevard
   Kansas City, Missouri 64110

   Batiked, ancient goddess, animal, and cave-painting inspired images on cotton clothing and T-shirts. To receive a free brochure, send a self-addressed stamped envelope.

Montana

Wild Womyn Wilderness Treks
   185 Red Dog Trail
   Darby, Montana 59829
   (406) 821-3763

   "Celebrating womynhood and exploring the magic of nature," since 1984. Group size is limited. Call or write for additional information.

New Jersey

Raven Recordings
   P.O. Box 2034, Drawer 37
   Red Bank, New Jersey 07701
   (201) 642-1979; (800) 76-RAVEN

   Call or write for a free catalog of tribal, primitive, trance and dance music by Gabrielle Roth and the Mirrors, Daniel Lauter/Suru Ekeh, Native Ground, Matt Balitsaris, and Nicolas.

New Mexico

La Caldera de Hekate
3212 Rio Grande N.W.
Albuquerque, New Mexico 87107
(505) 344-8484

An urban sanctuary dedicated to work in the areas of death and dying. Includes a Kiva and outdoor circle area. Holds regular ceremonial events. By appointment only.

New York

High Valley: A Place to Be
RR 2, Box 243
Sunset Trail
Clinton Corners, New York 12414
(914) 266-3621

A nonprofit retreat center staffed by practicing Pagans. Located on two hundred acres of sacred grove and open 365 days a year for all who wish to be connected to the Earth.

Kathleen's Bijoux
c/o Kathleen Kmen
HCR-1, Box 184
Malone, New York 12953
(518) 481-6705

Nestled in the most northern Adirondacks near Titus Mountain, Kathleen's Bijoux offers custom jewelry at affordable prices. Check out the handmade paper creations. Other possibilities include wood, bone, crystal, and more. *Bijoux* is French for gems or jewels, as well as that which is precious.

Rev. Maria Solomon
52 Libby Avenue
Hicksville, New York 11801
(516) 433-9118

Well-known author, TV and radio personality, and internationally known Hungarian psychic offers accurate, insightful readings through ancient methods, covering business, health, love, money, spirituality, and other topics via mail and telephone.

Pennsylvania

Katwood Sanctuary
c/o Changes Unlimited
34 E. State Street
Quarryville, Pennsylvania 17566
(804) 372-2810

A Pagan nature center on forty acres of field and forest, with sacred sites, organic gardens, a petting zoo, camping, bonfires, circles, and more. Accepts donations. By appointment only.

Tennessee

Dolls
P.O. Box 875
Madisonville, Tennessee 37354

Custom-made dolls celebrating the God and the Goddess, fantasy, mythological, historical, and operatic themes (including Wagner's "Ring"). To receive a catalog, send $3.00 to the above address.

Texas

The Brewers' Witch BBS
8880 Bellaire B-2, no. 139
Houston, Texas 77036
(713) 272-7346 (message); (713) 272-7350

A computer network serving the Pagan community of southern Texas.

Witchcraft Museum
107 E. Avenue E
Copperas Cove, Texas 76522

Vermont

Laurelin Retreat
RR 1, Box 239
Christian Hill Road
Bethal, Vermont 05032
(802) 234-9670

A spiritual retreat center providing sweat lodges, vision quests, weekend workshops and annual Church of Sacred Earth Summer Revels. By appointment only.

Virginia

Electronic Coven
222 W. 21st Street, no. F-145
Norfolk, Virginia 23517
(804) 625-5192

(Formerly Write Place BBS.) A Pagan-oriented computer network. Member of the national Pagan Information Net (P.I.N.). Twenty four hours.

Washington

Sew Mote It Be
P.O. Box 781
Bellingham, Washington 98227

Offers custom-made, handcrafted "spell coats." Each coat is available for $75.00 (includes shipping and handling). To order one for happiness, love, energy, or prosperity, send a photo of yourself, your color choice, size, and the spells you wish to have stitched into your reversible, unisex coat.

West Virginia

Mountain Vision, Inc.
P.O. Box 890
1290 Richwood Avenue
Morgantown, West Virginia 26505
(304) 296-3008; fax: (304) 296-3311

A meeting place for Pagan spiritual groups. Provides a social center, workshop, seminar, conference center and a metaphysical book-lending library.

United Kingdom (Scotland)

Dalriada BBS
  2 Brathwic Place
  Brodic, Isle of Arran KA 278 BN
  Scotland
  Phone: (40) 0770-302532

  Celtic heritage society, Rime Net, and Paganlink conference.

11

WHO'S WHO IN THE WICCAN COMMUNITY

In this section you will find the biographical profiles of some of the women and men (past and present) who, through their diverse talents and hard work, have contributed greatly to the Wiccan religion and helped shape it into what it is today. These Wiccans and Pagans, who are all magickal and beautiful in their own ways, deserve recognition for all the positive things they have done (and continue to do).

Unfortunately, some of these great individuals are no longer with us. Their passings were a great loss to the Wiccan community. However, although they may be gone, their achievements and contributions to the Craft are to be commended and surely will never be forgotten.

> "An it harm none, love,
> and do what thou wilt."

Blessed Be!

Cairril Adaire

Graphic designer and "Anarcho-Celtic" solitary Witch. Born: December 23, 1967. Founder and national coordinator for the Pagan Educational Network (PEN), founded in 1993 and dedicated to educating others about Paganism and building community. Publisher of *Water,* PEN's quarterly newsletter. Board member of the Wiccan Community Fund. Member of Environmental Defense Fund, Greenpeace, American Civil Liberties Union, Southern Poverty Law Center, Bloomington Feminist Chorus, and Institute for First Amendment Studies. Interests include: singing, music, his/herstory, politics and current events, feminism, writing, folklore, Celtic culture, civil rights and freedom issues, travel, Discordianism, science, anthropology, personal growth, and rites of passage. Mailing address: P.O. Box 1364, Bloomington, Indiana, 47402.

Margot Adler

Born: April 16, 1946, in Little Rock, Arkansas. She is a well-known and highly-respected Pagan, journalist, and lecturer. Education and degrees: B.A., University of California; M.S., Columbia University, Graduate School of Journalism; Nieman Fellow, Harvard University. Author of the popular book *Drawing Down the Moon* (1979, revised edition 1986).

Victor Anderson

Cofounder of the Faery Tradition of Wicca, he was born in New Mexico and initiated into the Craft at the age of nine. Author of *Thorns of the Blood Rose,* a book of Witchcraft-oriented poetry.

Clyde Anthony

Magickal-Wiccan name: Rajj. Poet, writer, and dancer. Born: February 16, 1934. Career includes professional dance and theater in San Francisco and New York City. Appeared on the March 1964 cover of *Dance Magazine.* His interests and talents range from trance-dancing to channeled poetry to dream-mediumship. Mailing address: P.O. Box 204, Monument Beach, Massachusetts 02553.

Rev. Paul V. Beyerl

Wiccan priest, author, and educator. Born: September 2, 1945, with a Virgo rising. Founder of the Rowan Tree Church, the Mystery School (teaching the Tradition of Lothlorien), *The Unicorn* newsletter (published since 1977), the Hermit's Grove, and the Hermit's Lantern. Well-known throughout the Neo-Pagan and Wiccan world, Beyerl's columns and articles have appeared in many publications. A guest speaker at many of the early Pagan gatherings, he has conducted seminars and workshops throughout the United States, and since 1986 has appeared annually as guest presenter at the Harvest Moon Celebration in Los Angeles. In addition to recognition as an herbalist and astrologer, Beyerl is known for his presentations on aspects of ritual, death and dying, ethics, alchemy, initiation, meditation, and visualization techniques, and for his performances of ritual that incorporate the skills of theater and music. Trained in classical music and the founder of the Unicorn Ensemble of Minneapolis (a chamber quartet), he is now retired from a ten-year career as a professional flutist. Author of *The Holy Books of the Devas* (1980, revised and expanded in 1993), *The Master Book of Herbalism* (1984), *A Wiccan Bardo: Initiation and Self-Transformation* (1989), *Painless Astrology* (1993), and *A Wiccan Reader* (1994). Mailing address: P.O. Box 0691, Kirkland, Washington 98083.

Isaac Bonewits

Druid priest, magician, and activist. Born: October 1, 1949, in Royal Oak, Michigan. Founder of the Aquarian Anti-Defamation League, Schismatic Druids of North America, and a Druidic fellowship known as Ar nDraiocht Fein. Established the *Druid Chronicler* in 1978 (later renamed *Pentalpha Journal*), and served as editor of *Gnostica* for one and one-half years. He holds a bachelor of arts in magic from the University of California at Berkeley, and is the author of *Real Magic* (1971) and *The Druid Chronicles (Evolved)*.

Goldie Brown

Astrologer and herbalist. Born: April 28, 1951, with a Gemini rising. Coven member and solitary practitioner of the Old Religion (Witchcraft), and Traditionalist. Member of Tuatha de Danaan

(Elder), Pittsburgh Pagan Alliance (coordinator and scribe), Fellowship of Isis, and Witches' Anti-Defamation League. Special talents, hobbies, and interests include astrology, herbs, runes, writing, publishing, music, sewing, gardening, ecology, and nature. Publisher of *Wyrd: Poetry Quarterly;* previously published *Rose Runes,* a Craft journal (1978–1981), and the *Owlet,* a Witches' newsletter (1975–1979). Mailing address: P.O. Box 624, Monroeville, Pennsylvania 15146.

Raymond Buckland

Born: August 31, 1934. Founder of the Seax-Wica tradition of Witchcraft. Educated at King's College School in London and holds a doctorate in anthropology from Brantridge Forest College in Sussex, England. Initiated into the Craft by Lady Olwen, the late Gerald Gardner's High Priestess. Established the first Museum of Witchcraft and Magic in the United States, and the Seax-Wica Seminary in the state of Virginia. Author of numerous books, including: *A Pocket Guide to the Supernatural* (1969), *Witchcraft Ancient and Modern* (1970), *Practical Candleburning Rituals* (1970), *Mu Revealed* (1970, under the pseudonym Tony Earll), *Witchcraft From the Inside* (1971), *The Tree: The Complete Book on Saxon Witchcraft* (1974), *Here is the Occult* (1974), *Amazing Secrets of the Psychic World* (1975), *Anatomy of the Occult* (1977), *The Magic of Chant-O-Matics* (1978), *Practical Color Magick* (1983), *Buckland's Complete Book of Witchcraft* (1986), and *Ray Buckland's Magic Cauldron* (1995).

Z. Budapest

Born: January 30, 1940, in Budapest. Founder and leader of the main branch of Feminist Dianic Wicca, also lecturer and presenter of workshops. Served as High Priestess of the Susan B. Anthony Coven (established in 1971 on the Winter Solstice) and the Laughing Goddess Coven. She directs the Women's Spirituality Forum in Oakland, California and works on a Goddess-oriented cable television program called *Thirteenth Heaven.* Author of *The Holy Book of Women's Mysteries* (two volumes). Mailing address: P.O. Box 11363, Oakland, California 94611.

Pauline and Dan Campanelli

Solitary Wiccan artists and authors. Interests include researching Mediterranean and Old European magick and Witchcraft, the origins of current holiday traditions, and the practice of Witchcraft. Authors of: *Wheel of the Year: Living the Magickal Life* (1989), *Ancient Ways: Reclaiming Pagan Traditions* (1991), *Circles, Groves and Sanctuaries* (1992), *Rites of Passage: The Pagan Wheel of Life* (1994), *Halloween Collectables* (1995), and *Romantic Valentines* (1996). Their paintings are reproduced by the New York Graphic Society and distributed worldwide. A book, *The Art of Pauline and Dan Campanelli* (New York Graphic Society, 1995), features their paintings and lifestyle. Mailing address: c/o Llewellyn Worldwide, P.O. Box 64383, St. Paul, Minnesota 55164.

Phil Catalano

Parapsychologist and engineering manager. Born: February 12, 1947. Solitary practitioner (Wiccan, Shamanic, Celtic). Holds a bachelor of science degree in parapsychology and is a member of IANS (International Association for New Science) and BOTA (Builders of the Adytum). Student with Occult Mystery School. Interests include UFOs, paranormal phenomena, sacred gemstones, magick, and metaphysics. Mailing address: P.O. Box 621165, Littleton, Colorado 80162.

Susann Cobb

Wiccan name: Peri Wyrrd. Born: January 7, 1963, with a Gemini rising. For more than ten years she has been involved in the book publishing community in the areas of sales and marketing; worked for leading metaphysical and health book publishers (Harper San Francisco and Inner Traditions). She is a member of E.S.C. (EarthSpirit Community), Earth Drum Council, and Moonfire Women's Spirituality Circles. Interests include Pagan gatherings, community outreach and education, and drumming as transformation. Mailing address: RR 1, Box 55, Rochester, Vermont 05767.

Arnold Crowther

English Witch, professional stage magician, founding member of the Puppet Guild, and a leading spokesperson for the Craft. Born:

October 7, 1909. Died: May 1, 1974. Author of *Let's Put on a Show* (1964), *Linda and the Lollipop Man* (1973), *Yorkshire Customs* (1974), and *Hex Certificate* (published in the late 1970s). Coauthor of *The Secrets of Ancient Witchcraft* (1974) and *The Witches Speak* (1976).

Patricia Crowther

English Witch, professional singer, magician, and puppeteer, and a leading spokesperson for the Craft through her books and lectures and the media. Author of *Witchcraft in Yorkshire, Witch Blood!, Lid Off the Cauldron,* and numerous articles that have appeared in such periodicals as *Prediction, Gnostica,* and *New Dimensions.* She is the coauthor of *The Secrets of Ancient Witchcraft* (1974) and *The Witches Speak* (1976). With her husband Arnold, she produced *A Spell of Witchcraft*—the first radio series about the Craft to air in Great Britain.

Scott Cunningham

Born: June 27, 1956, in Royal Oak, Michigan. Died: March 28, 1993. Cunningham was a prolific Wiccan writer and a practitioner of the Craft since 1971. He spoke at many lectures, taught groups across the country, and made occasional media appearances in an effort to dispel the misconceptions about Witchcraft and to educate the public about Wicca as a contemporary religion. Author of *Magical Herbalism* (1982), *Earth Power: Techniques of Natural Magic* (1983), *Cunningham's Encyclopedia of Magical Herbs* (1985), *The Magic of Incense, Oils and Brews* (1987), *The Magical Household* (1987, with David Harrington), *Cunningham's Encyclopedia of Crystal, Gem and Metal Magic* (1987), *The Truth About Witchcraft* (1988), and *Wicca: A Guide for the Solitary Practitioner* (1988). In addition to his books about Wicca and magick, he had twenty one published novels between 1980 and 1987.

Gerina Dunwich

Born: December 27, 1959, with a Taurus rising. Tradition: Eclectic Wicca and Neo-Classical Witchcraft; student of many occult arts, including the Tarot and other methods of divination, spirit-channeling, wortcunning, and past-life regression. Career: book author, editor, and publisher of *Golden Isis* since 1980, editor and publisher of *Pagan Pride*, professional astrologer, and antique shop proprietor. Founder of North Country Wicca, the Pagan Poets Society, Wheel of Wisdom School, and Coven Mandragora. Member of The Author's Guild, The Authors League of America, WPPA, Circle, and the Fellowship of Isis. She is also a member of the American Biographical Institute Board of Advisors and is listed in a number of reference works, such as *Who's Who in the East, Personalities of America*, and *Crossroads: Who's Who of the Magickal Community*. Author of *Candlelight Spells* (1988), *The Magick of Candleburning* (1989), *The Concise Lexicon of the Occult* (1990), *Circle of Shadows* (1990), *Wicca Craft* (1991), *The Secrets of Love Magick* (1992), *The Wicca Spellbook* (1994), *The Wicca Book of Days* (1995), *The Wicca Garden* (1996), *Words of the Cosmic Winds* (1996), and *The Wicca Source Book* (1996). In addition, her poetry and articles have been published in many journals, and she has been interviewed on numerous radio talk shows across the United States and Canada. Appeared as a guest speaker at the 1996 Craft Wise Pagan gathering in Waterbury, Connecticut. Mailing address: P.O. Box 525, Fort Covington, New York 12937.

Reed Morgan Dunwich

Writer, poet, and publisher of the *Silver Pentagram*, a Witchcraft journal. Born: February 2, 1948. A member of the Craft since 1965, he formed the Northern Star Coven in 1968 and continues to serve as its High Priest. He holds two bachelor of science degrees in psychology and computer science from the University of Pittsburgh and is a member of the Wiccan/Pagan Press Alliance, the Order of the Crystal Moon, the Pagan Poets Society, the Mathematical Association of America, and the Challenger Center for Space Science Education (founding member). Reed's poetry and articles have appeared in many Craft journals, including *Mystic Magick; Georgian Monthly; Converging Paths; Midnight Drive;* and *Golden Isis*. Interests and talents include astronomy, geology, math, and physics, reading books about the Craft, communicating intuitively with the Goddess, poetry, and dancing to rock music. Mailing address: P.O. Box 9776, Pittsburgh, Pennsylvania 15229.

Janet Farrar

Born: June 24, 1950, in London, England. Initiated into the Craft in 1970 by Alexander Sanders. With her husband Stewart, coauthor of many Witchcraft books: *Eight Sabbats for Witches* (1981), *The Witches' Way* (1984), *The Witches' Goddess* (1987), *Life and Times of a Modern Witch* (1987), and *The Witches' God* (1989).

Stewart Farrar

Born: June 28, 1916, in Highams Park, Essex, England. Educated at City of London School and University College, London. Served as president of the London University Journalism Union and was the editor of *London Union* magazine. Initiated into the Craft by Alexander Sanders. Coauthor of *Eight Sabbats for Witches* (1981), *The Witches' Way* (1984), *The Witches' Goddess* (1987), *Life and Times of a Modern Witch* (1987), and *The Witches' God* (1989). In addition to books on Witchcraft, Farrar is also the author of numerous occult novels and several detective novels.

Ed Fitch

Wiccan High Priest and key founder of the organization Pagan Way. Initiated into the Gardnerian tradition of the Craft by Raymond Buckland and his then-wife Rosemary. Published the *Crystal Well*, a magazine of neo-romantic Paganism. Interests and hobbies include Odinism, dance magick, and geomancy. Author of *The Grimoire of the Shadows; The Outer Court Book of Shadows;* and *Magical Rites From the Crystal Well* (1984).

Selena Fox

Well-known and respected founder and High Priestess of Circle Sanctuary, published author, and Pagan religious freedom activist. Born: October 20, 1949, in Arlington, Virginia. Attended the College of William and Mary and holds a bachelor of science degree in psychology. Selena is the founder of the Wiccan Shamanism Path of the Wiccan Religion. She also teaches, frequently speaks at lectures, and presents many workshops. In addition, she is a legally-recognized Wiccan minister and a leading spokesperson on the Craft to the media. Some of her interests and hobbies include herbcraft, dream-craft, healing, Goddess lore, Shamanism, chant-making, and singing. Mailing address: Box 219, Mt. Horeb, Wisconsin 53572.

Carolyn Frances

Poet, artist, composer, dancer. Born: April 19, 1942. Graduate of the Boston Museum School of Art, Modern and Mid-East Dancing. Composer of electronically-enhanced voice-sound works using channeled poetry and sounds of the environment. Mailing address: P.O. Box 204, Monument Beach, Massachusetts 02553.

Gavin Frost

Born in 1930 in Staffordshire, England. Graduated from London University with a bachelor of science degree in mathematics, and then a doctorate in physics and math. He also holds a doctor of divinity degree from the Church of Wicca. Cofounder of the Church and School of Wicca (1965) and author of more than a dozen books, including *The Witch's Bible* (1975), which he coauthored with his wife Yvonne.

Yvonne Frost

Born in Los Angeles, California, in 1931. Graduated from Fullerton Junior College in 1962 with an associate of arts degree in secretarial skills. Also holds a doctor of divinity degree from the Church of Wicca. Cofounder of the Church and School of Wicca (1965) and author of more than a dozen books, including *The Witch's Bible* (1975), which she coauthored with her husband Gavin.

Gerald B. Gardner

Founder of what came to be known as the Gardnerian Tradition which, in modern Witchcraft, is the dominant tradition. Born: June 13, 1884, in England. Died: February 12, 1964. Gardner is best remembered as the individual chiefly responsible for the Witchcraft revival in the modern West. The descendant of a Scottish Witch who was burned at the stake in 1610, Gardner was initiated into the Craft in 1939 by a woman called Old Dorothy Clutterbuck, the High Priestess of a New Forest coven. He was made an honorary member of the Ordo Templi Orientis by Aleister Crowley, and made numerous media appearances, enjoying the public spotlight in the 1950s and early 1960s. Author of several novels and the following nonfiction Craft books: *Witchcraft Today* (1954) and *The Meaning of Witchcraft* (1959).

Ellen Evert Hopman

Magickal name: Willow. Born: July 31, 1952, with a Capricorn rising. She is a master herbalist and lay homeopath who holds a master of education degree in mental health counseling. In addition, she teaches, holds workshops, and works as a counselor and a tour guide to sacred sites of Europe. She is a Bard of the Gorsedd of Caer Abiri in Avebury, England; vice president of Keltria, the International Druid Fellowship; and a professional member of the American Herbalists Guild. Other memberships include the Nature Conservancy, Author's Guild, Druid Clan of Dana; Order of Bards, Ovates and Druids; Order of the White Oak, Maple Dragon Clan of Vermont, and North East Herb Association. Author of *People of the Earth—The New Pagans Speak Out; Tree Medicine, Tree Magic; A Druid's Herbal for the Sacred Earth Year;* and the video *Gifts of the Healing Earth.* Mailing address: P.O. Box 219, Amherst, Massachusetts 01004.

Jade

Born: July 2, 1950 (Gemini rising). Creator of the Women's Thealogical Institute, Cella Training Program (the first institute offering an in-depth training course for women wishing to be ordained priestesses.) Author of *To Know: A Guide to Women's Magic and Spirituality.* Cofounder of the Re-formed Congregation of the Goddess—the first legally incorporated tax-exempt religion serving the women's spiritual community. Cofounder and coordinator of *Of a Like Mind,* the largest women's newspaper and network exploring Goddess spirituality for women. Copublisher of *Solitary: By Choice or by Chance,* a journal for those who practice the Craft alone. Vocal recording artist with Triple Crescent, a Goddess-oriented musical group. Jade has spoken and sung widely about women's spirituality and Dianic Wicca. She is an outstanding presenter and public speaker with an extensive knowledge of Feminist Witchcraft. Mailing address· P.O. Box 6677, Madison, Wisconsin, 53716.

Rik Johnson

Born: August 24, 1952. Gardnerian Wiccan and High Priest of the Desert Henge Coven (formed April 1982, one of the oldest covens in the state of Arizona). First and Second Degree Gardnerian, Third Degree Traditional (done by an Alexandrian but not an Alexandrian Elevation; seeking Third Degree Gardnerian.) Occupations: clerk in legal system, also Arizona National Guard civil engineer. Won civil rights victory by forcing the Air Force to list his religion as Wicca. Performs legalized handfastings in Arizona and teaches the oldest public class on Wicca in that state. Consulted by police in "occult" crimes. Lectured at the University of Arizona. Helped the police academy form a class on how a police officer should deal with Witches. Facilitated the Tucson area Wiccan Network (1995), performed numerous public rituals for the TAWN Fall Fest. Published in numerous newsletters. Enjoys collecting Craft-related material such as term papers, news articles, videos, and music. Constantly seeking material on Wicca to be used for public classes and currently working on a Wiccan songbook, a Wiccan humor book, a technical manual on magick, and a book entitled *Theology of Witchcraft*. Mailing address: P.O. Box 40451, Tucson, Arizona 85717.

Anodea Judith

Founder and Director of Lifeways, charter member of Forever Forests, president of Church of All Worlds. Born: December 1, 1952. Educated at Clark University, the California College of Arts and Crafts in Oakland, California, and John F. Kennedy University. The sister of comedian Martin Mull, Judith is an artist and songwriter, and helps others through her work as a professional therapist. Interests include Witchcraft and magick, psychic development, ecology, bioenergetic therapy, chakras, theater, and art. Author of *Wheels of Life: A User's Guide to the Chakras* (1987) and accompanying tape.

G. M. Kelly

Writer and novelist, editor of *The Newaeon Newsletter* (established in 1977). Born: March 23, 1951, with a Pisces rising and Moon in Libra. Magickal name: Frater Keallach 93/676. "No special 'talents,' psychic or otherwise, certainly not very good at making money appear—blast my ethics and integrity!" Interests include Tarot, ⲅ

Ching, Thelema, Aleister Crowley, Magic/k (both ceremonial and "tantric"), the Old West, Native Americans, the American Civil War, and numerous other things. Author of *Grimm Justice: A Mythological Western; Sins of the Flesh;* and various short stories published under pseudonyms. "However, my most impressive accomplishment to date is that I have survived almost forty-five years now in a hostile social and economic environment and even more impressive, my sense of humor is intact." Mailing address: P.O. Box 19210, Pittsburgh, Pennsylvania 15213.

Lady Sheba

Famous Witch Queen and psychic. Born in the mountains of Kentucky (birthdate unknown) to a family whose religious and magickal link to the Craft spanned seven generations. She was introduced to the Old Religion by her grandmother and initiated as a Witch in the 1930s. Founder and High Priestess of the American Order of the Brotherhood of Wicca. Author of *The Magick Grimoire* and *The Book of Shadows* (1971).

Sybil Leek

Born: February 22, 1917, in Stoke-on-Trent, England. Died: October 26, 1982, in Melbourne, Florida. Miss Leek moved to the United States in the early 1960s and achieved fame and success as a modern Witch, astrologer, and occult author. Her psychic predictions of the Kennedy assassinations and the election of Richard M. Nixon as president of the United States are documented. Edited and published her own astrological journal and wrote an internationally syndicated column. Author of over sixty books, including the bestselling *Diary of a Witch* (1968).

Dr. Leo Louis Martello

Magickal name: Nemesis. Witch, graphologist, lecturer, book author, and activist for both civil and gay rights. Born in Dudley, Massachusetts, under the sign of Libra. Martello has been publicly prominent in the modern Witchcraft movement since the 1960s. Educated at Assumption College in Worcester, Massachusetts, the Institute for Psychotherapy in New York City, and Hunter College in New York

City. He holds a doctor of divinity degree from the National Congress of Spiritual Consultants, is an ordained minister (Spiritual Independents, nonsectarian), and served as pastor of the Temple of Spiritual Guidance from 1955 to 1960. Founder and director of the American Hypnotism Academy in New York (1950-1954); treasurer of the American Graphological Society (1955-1957). Sponsored a public "Witch-In" in New York City's Central Park on Halloween/Samhain in 1970. Founder and director of the Witches Anti-Defamation League. Interests include: treasure-hunting, handwriting analysis, and dreams. Author of numerous magazine articles and books, including: *Witchcraft: The Old Religion; Black Magic, Satanism and Voodoo; Understanding the Tarot; It's Written in the Cards; What It Means to Be a Witch; Weird Ways of Witchcraft; It's Written in the Stars; Curses in Verses; Witches' Liberation and Practical Guide to Witch Covens; Your Pen Personality;* and *The Hidden World of Hypnotism.* He also wrote the introductions for the following books: *Secrets of Ancient Witchcraft and Witches' Tarot* (Crowther); *The Witches Speak* (Crowther); *Witch Blood!* (Crowther); and *The Meaning of Witchcraft* (Gardner).

Leila Moon

Solitary Witch and spiritual specialist. Born: June 15, 1966, with an Aries rising. Writes horoscopes for the Craft periodical *Spinning in the Light.* Interests and talents include psychic Tarot-channeling, palmistry, crystal healing, candle magick and aromatherapy. "Initiated by the Golden Dawn and completing initiation for Vodon. As we gain and develop in our priesthood of spiritual knowledge, we pass on to those who are in need of spiritual help." Mailing address: 1725 E. Charleston Street, Las Vegas, Nevada 89104.

Karin Muller

Licensed minister, licensed practical nurse, desktop publisher, ceremonialist-Shaman. Born: December 26, 1964, with a Libra rising. Solitary Wiccan (apprentice to Feri). Founder and director of the Full Circle Center for Spiritual and Community Development. Coordinator and leader of several large Pagan rituals annually in her local area. Publishes the quarterly *Anamnesia,* serving the Pagan community of western Massachusetts and beyond. Bachelor of arts in women, spirituality and power from Mount Holyoke College, where her thesis work examined the feminist Witchcraft movement in the Pioneer Valley. Talents and interests include some Shamanic healing, public ritual, women's spirituality, and empowerment. Mailing address: 37 Clark Road, Cummington, Massachusetts 01026.

John Opsopaus

Magickal name: Apolonius Sophistes. Solitary practitioner of the Hellenic Tradition. Occupation: computer scientist. Member of Church of All Worlds, Ar nDraiocht Fein and O.T.O. Published articles include "Hellenic Neopaganism," "Neoclassical Sacrifice," "Rotation of the Elements," a Hellenic version of the Lesser Banishing Ritual, and various hymns to goddesses and gods. Maintains several Worldwide Web sites devoted to Hellenic Neo-Paganism and the occult, including the Pythagorean Tarot. Runs the Omphalos networking service for Neo-Pagans following Greek and Roman traditions. Interests and talents include divination (Tarot, I Ching, dice oracles, alphabet oracles), ancient numerology, ancient music, mythology, ritual construction, alchemy, and archetypal psychology. Mailing address: UT Box 16220, Knoxville, Tennessee 37996.

Pete Pathfinder

Born under the sign of Aries. Founder of both the Aquarian Tabernacle Church and the Center for Non-Traditional Religion. Cofounder and publisher of the journal *Panegyria*. In 1985 he served as public information officer for the Covenant of the Goddess. Originated the Dial-A-Pagan telephone information service (206-LA-PAGAN). Mailing address: P.O. Box 409, Index, Washington 98256.

Lee Prosser

Solitary practitioner of Shamanism and Vedanta. Occupation: researcher. Born: December 31, 1944. Founder of the Oneness Center for Spiritual Living; legally-recognized Interfaith minister; member of the Pagan Poets Society Education: prelaw at California State

University at Northridge; undergraduate degrees in English and sociology; master's degree in social science. Numerous publications since 1963. "To share knowledge that will aid a person on the personal path to self-knowledge and self-discovery is one of the best gifts you can give that person. Self-knowledge is the key to enlightenment." Interested in Shamanic covens, Hindu magick, Hindu mythology, and all aspects of the Hindu goddess Durga. Author of *Desert Woman Visions: 100 Poems* (1987), and *Running From the Hunter* (1996). "I have held a lifelong interest in Wicca, Vedanta, Shamanism. Additionally have done research in early Christianity and early Pagan religions. One of my beliefs is found in the *Rig Veda:* Truth is One: Sages call it by various names." Mailing address: P.O. Box 185 Oologah, Oklahoma 74053.

Silver Ravenwolf

Born: September 11, 1956, with a Gemini rising. Clan Head of The Temple of the Morrighan Triskele (Black Forest Tradition, founded in 1991). Director of International Wiccan/Pagan Press Alliance; Director of Witches Anti-Discrimination League. Interests include criminal magick and divination. Major contributor to *The Magickal Almanac* (1994, 1995, 1996, and 1997) and author of *To Ride a Silver Broomstick; Hexcraft: Pennsylvania Dutch Magick; Beneath a Mountain Moon; To Stir a Magick Cauldron;* and *Angels, Companions in Magick.* Mailing address: P.O. Box 1392, Mechanicsburg, Pennsylvania 17055.

Deirdre Sargent

Born: October 14 (Scorpio rising). Solitary Wiccan and member of Wolf's Head Coven (formed in 1993). First officer, the Educational Society for Pagans; Elder at Large, Covenant of the Goddess, National Board. Coeditor of *Pagan Digest;* articles published in *Pagan Digest, Pallas Society News, Unicorn, Maypole,* and other publications. Provides classes and lectures to both the Pagan and cowan communities on a wide variety of metaphysical and scholarly subjects. Occupations: MIS systems analyst and actor (stage, Shakespearean). Interests include religious studies with emphasis on the early saints of the Christian church and their links to Paganism, the Templar Knights, and the Masonic connection to modern Witchcraft, and the phenomenon of human sacrifice past and present in Mesoamerica.

Herman Slater

Magickal name: Govannan. Wiccan High Priest and public advocate for the Craft. Initiated into the New York Coven of Welsh Traditional Witches in 1972. Proprietor of the Warlock Shop in New York City (which later changed its business name to the Magickal Childe.) Slater hosted a weekly cable television show called *The Magickal Mystery Tour*, which aired in Manhattan in 1987. Author of *A Book of Pagan Rituals, The Magickal Formulary,* and *The Magickal Formulary II*. Date of death: July 9, 1992.

Rev. Maria Solomon

Professional psychic, ordained minister, occultist, hypnotherapist, writer, lecturer, teacher, parapsychologist, and Shaman. Born: August 11, 1950. Founder of the Sylvan Society; member of the New York–New Jersey Psychic Guild, Floating Healing Meditation Circle, Hungarian Writers Guild, NAFE, Long Island Dowsing Association, and A.A.H. Honorable member of the Tuscarora Indian Tribe. Interests and talents include rune casting, Tarot trance, spiritual work, past lives, healing, candles, herbs, oils, spellcraft, Kirlian photography, biorhythms, astral projection, numerology, graphology, palmistry, psychometry, crystals and stones, Hatha Yoga, Tai chi, and Qi Gong. "My father is a psychic. Both my grandparents on my mother's side were spiritualist trance mediums. My grandfather also did automatic writing. My mother has a feel for herbs. My favorite colors are yellow, pink, and orange." Author of *Psychic Vibrations of Crystals, Gems and Stones; New Age Formulary;* and *Maria Solomon's Money Empowerment*. Numerous articles published in *Nightingale News, Ghost Trackers, ULC News, Innerlight, Gnostic Times, UFO Universe, The Alternative, Psychic Fair Network News,* and *Psychic Press*. Guest appearances on radio, television, cable and satellite TV. Conducted psychic fairs and ran a nationwide metaphysical catalog Goals: "To assist people internationally and teach them how to attain higher awareness of their true selves." Mailing address: 52 Libby Avenue. Hicksville, New York 11801.

Rainbow Star

Musician and member of Rainbow Link Coven (established in 1985). Traditions: Druid, Greek, Roman, and Faery. Born under the sign of Libra with a Leo rising. Member of Ar nDraiocht Fein. Interests include herbalism, Tarot, and music. Goals: "Heal the Earth, heal all waters, heal the air, heal all spirits, create joy!" Mailing address: P.O. Box 1218, Greenville, Mississippi 38702.

Starhawk

Feminist Witch, book author, and peace activist. Born in 1951. Initiated into the Faery Tradition. Founder of the Compost and Honeysuckle covens and Reclaiming (a feminist collective based in San Francisco.) She teaches at several colleges in the Bay Area and travels throughout the United States and abroad giving lectures and workshops. Author of *The Spiral Dance: A Rebirth of the Ancient Religion of the Great Goddess* (1979), *Dreaming in the Dark* (1982), and *Truth or Dare: Encounters of Power, Authority and Mystery* (1987).

Tarostar

Born under the sign of Aries. Education: University of Las Vegas; Kent State University, Ohio; Defense Language Institute, Monterey, California. Numerous articles published in *Georgian Newsletter* (Bakersfield, California). Lectures on Tarot, demonology and the Craft. Author of *The Sacred Pentagram; The Witch's Formulary and Spellbook;* and *The Witch's Spellcraft.*

Lady Tareena

Born: January 23, 1947. Accountant and editor. Member of Guardians of Light and Life (formed in 1990), Clan of the Spider—Universal Life Church. Talents and interests include: psychic channeling, Tarot, and astral journeys. She is a Priestess of Isis as well as an honorary Zulu Sangomo, and has many other honorary titles within the world's cultures. She has studied many religious cultures from all corners of the Earth, and holds six different business degrees. Through all of her studies the one thing that mattered most has been her ability and desire to help others learn and understand the intricacies of life and spirit. Mailing address: Spinning in the Light, 850 S. Rancho Drive, no. 2-355, Las Vegas, Nevada 89106.

Tony Taylor

Computer network specialist and Keltrian Druid. Born: July 27, 1950, with a Leo rising. Member of the Caer Duir grove (established in 1988), Henge of Keltria, Ar nDraiocht Fein, and The Order of Bards, Ovates, and Druids OBOD. Cofounder of The Henge of Keltria; editor-in-chief of *Keltria: Journal of Druidism and Celtic Magick.* Mailing address: c/o Henge of Keltria, P.O. Box 48369, Minneapolis, Minnesota 55448.

Patricia Telesco

Magickal name: LoreSinger. Professional writer and administrative assistant, part-time herbalist. Born: February 21, 1960. Solitary (eclectic and Kitchen Witchery) and member of Tempio della Stregheria. Coordinator of Metaphysical Artists for Gaia, a networking cooperative of writers, illustrators, and craftspeople with a quarterly newsletter, *Abracadabra.* Coordinated the *Magi* newsletter for four years; trustee for the Universal Federation of Pagans. Taped a segment for the show *Home Matters* (Discovery Channel, September 1993). Member of the Society for Creative Anachronism. Has given numerous lectures and workshops across the country. Numerous articles published and author of *A Victorian Grimoire* (1992), *The Urban Pagan* (1993), *A Victorian Flower Oracle* (1994), *Kitchen Witch's Cookbook* (1994), *A Witch's Brew* (1995), *Folklore, Fantasy, Fiction* (1995), and *Folkways* (1995). Contributor to *The Magical Almanac* (1994 editor, 1995, 1996, and 1997) and the *Llewellyn Moon Sign Book* (1994, 1995, 1996). Interests include: animal card, rune, flower, and oracle readings, cookery magick, carving wands, brewing ritual wines, and good fellowship. Also interested in magickal teachings for children. Goals: "To find more mainstream publishers with whom I can work to educate the public on magickal and New Age traditions." Mailing address: 492 Breckenridge Street, Buffalo, New York 14213.

Michael Thorn

Registered nurse and leader of the Kathexis Coven (established 1982, Gardnerian.) Member and former president of Covenant of the Goddess. Interests include gay spirituality and ceremonial magick. Author of *Wiccan Resources: A Guide to the Witchcraft Community.* Mailing address: P.O. Box 408, Shirley, New York 11967.

Doreen Valiente

English High Priestess of the Craft, poet, and a woman considered by many to be one of the most influential Witches of modern times. Author of numerous articles and the following books: *Natural Magic* (1975), *An ABC of Witchcraft Past and Present* (1973), and *Witchcraft for Tomorrow* (1978). She lives in Sussex, England.

Apophis Samhain Valkyrie

Writer and Wiccan minister. Born: September 27, 1969. "I am the founder of the Occulterian Life Church located in the Athens-Wausau, Wisconsin, area. I have been involved in Nature Spirituality all of my life." Author of *Wicca Unchained* and *Bats, Cats and Broomsticks: A Guide to Wiccan Tolerance and Understanding* (church published). "My interests include the forming of a newsletter-journal where correspondence from a variety of churches and organizations (Wiccan-Pagan) can be dispersed, discussed, and known. The Pagan community needs a more formal communicational networking among various groups to where others of the Pagan audience may know 'what's what' in their community." Mailing address: P.O. Box K, Athens, Wisconsin 54411.

Susun S. Weed

Born: February 8, 1946 with an Aquarius rising. Magickal/ Wiccan name: Lady Iona. Green Witch, author, educator. She is the founder of the Wise Woman Center in Woodstock, New York, editor-in-chief of Ash Tree Publishing, and the creator of the Amazon Tarot Deck. Author of *Wise Woman Herbal for the Childbearing Years* (1987), *Healing Wise* (1990), *Menopausal Years the Wise Woman Way* (1993), *Breast Cancer? Breast Health! the Wise Woman Way* (1996). Interests and talents include herbal medicine, Tarot, color and sound healing, Shamanic journeys, talking with plants, animal totems, earth attunement, and energy healing. Susun describes herself as a "gardener, goat herd, cheesemaker, sock knitter and friend of the fairies." Mailing address: P.O. Box 64, Woodstock, New York 12498

Marion Weinstein

Book author, entertainer, and media spokesperson for the modern Witchcraft movement. Graduated from Bernard College with a bachelor's degree in English literature. Studied film at Columbia University and worked in Los Angeles as a commercial artist and animator. She also studied acting, dance, and voice. Hosted a radio program in New York City called *Marion's Cauldron,* which aired regularly on radio station WBAI-FM (1969–1983). Formed Earth Magic Productions in 1979, which launched a quarterly newsletter in 1988 called the *Earth Magic Times.* Author of *Positive Magic* (1978), *Earth Magic: A Dianic Book of Shadows* (1979), *Racewalking* (1986), and *Remember the Goddess* (1989).

Carl Llewellyn Weschcke

Magickal name: Gnosticus. Book publisher, president of Llewellyn Worldwide and early publisher of Wiccan books. Born: September 10, 1930, with a Pisces rising. Solitary practitioner of Wicca (Celtic Tradition). Member of the ACLU, NAACP and AFA. Interests include Witchcraft, Shamanism, Tantra, ceremonial magick, Qabalah, and meditation. Mailing address: P.O. Box 64383, St. Paul, Minnesota 55164.

Morning Glory Zell

Born: May 27, 1947. She did her first vision quest in 1968. Studied Wicca, Celtic Shamanism, and Goddess history. Ordained as a Priestess in the Church of All Worlds in 1974; founded the Ecosophical Research Association in 1977. Helped develop a sacred wilderness retreat and the Living Unicorn project. Traveled, lectured, and taught college courses with her husband Oberon on Neo-Paganism, the Gaia Hypothesis, and Goddess reemergence. She is a Goddess historian, lore mistress, and Priestess of Potnia Theron. Took formal training with Joanna Macy and John Seed as a presenter for the Council of All Beings in 1990. Published two short stories from her "Tales of the Verdeveldt" cycle in Marion Zimmer Bradley's *Sword and Sorceress* anthologies; currently working on a book to be titled *A Gospel of Gaia.* Morning Glory is also the manufacturer, business manager, and proprietor of Mythic Images, which produces museum-quality replicas of ancient goddesses and gods sculpted in partnership with Oberon. Mailing address: P.O. Box 982, Ukiah, California 95482.

Oberon Zell

Born: November 30, 1942, with an Aquarius rising. Publisher of *Green Egg* magazine; sculptor for Mythic Images; Priest of the Church of All Worlds. Talents include those of: ritualist, workshop presenter, mediator and counselor, artist (especially sculpture and graphics), writer, thealogian, magician. Hobbies: paper masks, plastic models, scuba diving, sex, reading, and movies. Interested in cosmology, dinosaurs, archaeology, science fiction (especially *Star Trek* and *Babylon 5* on TV), ancient history, sex, nature, Gaia, goddesses, cryptozoology, and Shamanism. Founded the Church of All Worlds in 1962. Incorporated in 1968, it became the first Neo-Pagan church to obtain full federal recognition in the United States. As the first to apply the terms *Pagan* and *Neo-Pagan* to the newly emerging nature religions of the 1960s and through his publication of *Green Egg* (1968–1975; 1988–present), Oberon was instrumental in the coalescence of the Neo-Pagan movement. In 1970 Oberon formulated and published the theology of deep ecology, which has become known scientifically as the Gaia Thesis. With his soul mate Morning Glory, he founded the Ecosophical Research Association, whose projects have included raising unicorns, chasing mermaids, visiting ancient sacred sites, and exploring the underworld. Oberon is currently working on a book to be titled *The Gospel of Gaea*. Voted Favorite Pagan Writer in 1992; given the Silver Broomstick Award in 1994; *Green Egg* winner of the WPPA Gold Award in 1992, 1994, and 1995, and WPPA Bronze Award in 1993. Featured in many books, especially *Drawing Down the Moon; The Pagan Path; Encyclopedia of Witches and Witchcraft; Witchcraft: The Old Religion; People of the Earth: The New Pagans Speak Out,* and others. Mailing address: P.O. Box 982, Ukiah, California 95482.

12

Recommended Reading

Books About Wicca, Goddess Religion, Earth Spirituality, and Contemporary Paganism

Adler, Margot. *Drawing Down the Moon: Witches, Druids, Goddess-Worshippers, and Other Pagans in America Today.* Boston: Beacon Press, 1986. An excellent source on contemporary Paganism from Feminist Wicca to Men's Spirituality. Contains a resource guide to Pagan gatherings and festivals, periodicals, and organizations.

Andrews, Ted. *Animal-Speak: The Spiritual and Magical Powers of Creatures Great and Small.* St. Paul: Llewellyn, 1993. From dreams to earthly sightings, this comprehensive book details many meanings of birds, animals, insects, and reptiles.

Buckland, Raymond. *Buckland's Complete Book of Witchcraft.* St. Paul: Llewellyn, 1986. This is an excellent Witchcraft book for beginners.

Budapest, Zsuzsanna. *The Holy Book of Women's Mysteries.* Oakland, Calif.: Wingbow Press, 1989. Perfect for the Goddess in every woman: healing, blessings, celebrations, divination, and much more.

Campanelli, Dan, and Pauline Campanelli. *Circles, Groves and Sanctuaries.* St. Paul: Llewellyn, 1992. Focuses on the sacred spaces of today's Pagans. Illustrated with over 115 inspiring photographs.

Campanelli, Pauline. *Wheel of the Year: Living the Magickal Life.* St. Paul: Llewellyn, 1993. Seasonal rituals and charms for the Sabbats and the long weeks between them. Coven Mandragora and I have performed a few of the rituals in this fine book and have found them to be very beautiful and most enjoyable.

Crowther, Arnold, and Patricia Crowther. *The Secrets of Ancient Witchcraft.* New York: Citadel Press, 1974. A great book for both the novice and the seasoned Witch. Traces many modern religious customs back to their prehistoric Pagan origins. Offers Sabbat ceremonies (which are ideal in their present form for solitary practitioners or easily adapted for coven use) and explains the meanings of the Witches Tarot (which was created by Arnold Crowther for use in the circle and based upon Witchcraft symbolism.)

Eisler, Riane. *The Chalice and the Blade.* New York: Harper and Row, 1987. If you are not already angered by and working to reverse thousands of years of patriarchal ravaging, then strap yourself in for the ultimate shift in perspective. Your life may never be the same after reading this.

Farrar, Janet, and Stewart Farrar. *The Witches' Goddess: The Feminine Principle of Divinity.* Custer, Wash.: Phoenix Publishing, 1987. This book offers an excellent overview of the Goddess as She was worshipped in ancient times throughout Western Europe and the Near East. Rituals to invoke Celtic and Mediterranean goddesses as well as a comprehensive list of goddesses from nearly every culture around the world are also included.

Fitzgerald, Waverly. *School of the Seasons: Aligning With the Rhythms of the Earth.* Seattle: Priestess of Swords Press, 1993. A wonderful book that serves as an introduction to the correspondence course, *School of the Seasons.* Offers powerful suggestions for honoring our cycles.

Guiley, Rosemary Ellen. *The Encyclopedia of Witches and Witchcraft.* New York: Facts on File, 1989. A must for every Witch's personal library! Highly informative and well illustrated. Covers both ancient Witchcraft and contemporary Wicca. Also contains interesting profiles and photos of numerous and well-known modern Witches.

Guiley, Rosemary Ellen. *Harper's Encyclopedia of Mystical and Paranormal Experience.* San Francisco: Harper San Francisco, 1991. More than five hundred cross-related entries. An excellent educational source for Witches, Shamans, students of the occult arts, and all who are interested in the New Age. Lavishly illustrated.

Harris, Maria. *Dance of the Spirit.* New York: Bantam Books, 1989. The seven steps of women's spirituality are presented in a way that will appeal to women of all persuasions.

Hopman, Ellen Evert, and Lawrence Bond. *People of the Earth: The New Pagans Speak Out.* Rochester, Vt.: Destiny Books, 1996. A fascinating collection of interviews with a variety of contemporary Pagan leaders and teachers. Also contains photographs and a resource section.

Morwyn. *Secrets of a Witch's Coven.* West Chester, Penn.: Whitford Press, 1988. Very informative and an ideal book for the novice Witch. Presents the modern Craft in a positive light.

O'Gaea, Ashleen. *The Family Wicca Book.* St. Paul: Llewellyn. Highly recommended for Wiccans and Witches who are raising (or planning to raise) their children in the Craft. Addresses the needs and experiences of the Wiccan family.

Sjoo, Monica, and Barbara Mor. *The Great Cosmic Mother: Rediscovering the Religion of the Earth.* San Francisco: Harper and Row, 1987. Traces the history and worship of the Great Goddess from a modern feminist perspective. Discusses Her various symbols and sacred images, moon and blood mysteries, the persecution of Witches, and the recent economic exploitation of global militarism, among other things. Informative and very thought-provoking.

Starhawk. *The Spiral Dance.* San Francisco: Harper and Row, 1979. One of the first (and best) textbooks on Goddess spirituality, offering meditations, rituals, and spells. Highly recommended for all who seek the path of the Goddess.

Books About Herbs and Wortcunning

Beyerl, Paul. *The Master Book of Herbalism.* Custer, Wash.: Phoenix Publishing, 1984. An excellent and very informative book for all who are interested in the healing and ritual use of herbs.

Cunningham, Scott. *Cunningham's Encyclopedia of Magical Herbs.* St. Paul: Llewellyn, 1985. An illustrated collection of over four hundred magickal herbs from A to Z. In my opinion, this is one of the finest herbal reference books on the market today. It is fully indexed and cross-indexed by name, common names, use, and rulership.

Hylton, William H., ed. *The Rodale Herb Book.* Emmaus, Penn.: Rodale Press, 1974. Although this is not officially a "Witchcraft book," throughout its pages you will find numerous references to Witches and their connections to various plants. This book mainly focuses on the medicinal use of herbs; however, it also offers recipes and instructions for making herbal potpourri, plant dyes, and more.

Books About Magick and the Divinatory Arts

Almond, Jocelyn, and Keith Seddon. *Understanding Tarot.* London: Aquarian Press, 1991.

Fitch, Ed, and Janine Renee. *Magical Rites From the Crystal Well.* St. Paul: Llewellyn, 1984.

Greer, Mary K. *The Essence of Magic: Tarot, Ritual, and Aromatherapy.* Van Nuys, Calif.: Newcastle Publishing Company, 1993. A wonderful introduction to scent and evoking the powers represented by the Major Arcana. This book also includes Tarot spreads and some numerology with regard to personal destiny.

Hope, Murry. *Practical Greek Magic.* London: Aquarian Press, 1985. An excellent description of the theory of Greek magick and its practical application.

Konraad, Sandor. *Classic Tarot Spreads.* West Chester, Penn.: Whitford Press, 1985. Recommended for both the novice and experienced card reader. Includes twenty two classic spreads.

Noble, Vicki. *Motherpeace: A Way to the Goddess Through Myth, Art, and Tarot.* New York: HarperCollins, 1983. Accompaniment to the Motherpeace Tarot Cards, this book offers a feminist perspective and feminine-empowering version of the Tarot.

Slater, Herman. *A Book of Pagan Rituals.* York Beach, Maine: Samuel Weiser, 1978.

Stein, Diane. *The Women's Book of Healing.* St. Paul: Llewellyn, 1987. Ways of using gemstones, chakras, and the laying on of hands are explored, as well as other ways of curing disease.

Telesco, Patricia. *Spinning Spells, Weaving Wonders.* Freedom, Calif.: The Crossing Press, 1996. Arranged alphabetically by topic, over three hundred spells for nearly every positive purpose imaginable are contained in this book. Also included are appendixes for magickal associations, Pagan deities, and handcrafting various items for use in spellcraft.

Telesco, Patricia. *The Victorian Flower Oracle.* St. Paul: Llewellyn, 1994. This is a beautiful book that teaches the secrets of using flowers to reveal the future. It includes easy-to-understand instructions for making a flower deck from pressed flowers or artwork, as well as the divinatory meanings of numerous flowers, herbs, and trees.

Books About Astrology

Llewellyn's Moon Sign Book and Lunar Planning Guide. Published annually by Llewellyn Publications (St. Paul, Minn.), this is a great book for helping to determine the astrologically ideal dates for almost any activity (such as gardening, fishing, buying or selling, legal or business matters, or gambling). Weather and earthquake forecasts, predictions of world events, and monthly horoscopes are also included in this reliable reference source. Llewellyn also publishes the annual *Sun Sign Book,* which offers detailed personal horoscopes for all twelve signs; the *Daily Planetary Guide* (an annual astrology datebook); and a full-color astrological calendar containing a fifteen-month retrograde table, monthly horoscopes, a lunar planting guide, and much more. Highly recommended for the professional astrologer as well as the novice stargazer and anyone interested in the mystical science of the stars.

Sakoian, Frances, and Louis S. Acker. *The Astrologer's Handbook.* New York: Harper and Row, 1989. One of the most comprehensive astrology books ever published. Includes complete instructions for interpreting any natal chart and easy-to-follow directions for casting your own charts.

Index